Bob Moats

I0567267

Vegas Vigilante Murders

By Bob Moats
Re-edited March 2013

Rev. 0410141105

1

Vegas Vigilante Murders

ISBN – 978-0-9903138-3-0

For information and address:
Magic 1 Productions
P.O. Box 524, Fraser MI 48026-0524
Website: http://murdernovels.com
Cover by Bob Moats

Bob Moats

Other Jim Richards series books by Bob Moats

(In Series Order)
Classmate Murders
Vegas Showgirl Murders
Dominatrix Murders
Mistress Murders
Bridezilla Murders
Magic Murders
Strip Club Murders
Made-for-TV Murders
Mystery Cruise Murders
Talk Show Murders
Sin City Murders
Black Widow Murders
Vegas Vigilante Murders
Area 51 Murders
Mortuary Murders
Hypnotic Murders
Sunshine State Murders
Blue Suede Murders
Honky Tonk Murders
Dark Carnival Murders
Lipstick Murders
Pasta Murders
Talent Show Murders
Shyster Murders
Campground Murders
Network Murders
Reunion Murders
Big Apple Murders
Kennel Murders
Trick or Treat Murders
Santa Murders
Wiseguy Murders

For a preview or to purchase a book, go to
http://murdernovels.com

What people are saying about the Murder Novels by Bob Moats

"Every now and again you stumble upon something wonderful on the internet. Bob Moats' "Classmate Murders" is an excellent blend of Elmore Leonard and Philip Marlowe sensibilities, with an unexpected hero well into his sixties, downsized from his job and forced into an early retirement he can't afford. The character is easy to relate to, the story itself a wonderful suspenseful ride with a cast of interesting characters, and damn if it isn't some great detective writing. If you like your crime novels gritty, with a touch of biker sensibility and a side of arthritis, you'll love Bob Moat's work."
Review by M. Jones, author "314 CRESCENT MANOR"

"I went online this morning and read your book. I thought at first that I would only read a few pages, but got sucked into it and read all 11 chapters. You are a very good writer! I read quite a bit and often pick up "Airport" paperback mysteries to read on a plane. Most of them are dreadful, with obvious plots. Classmate Murders is a much better story than most."
Ray Zink, Entrepreneur, Minn.

"I got up to chapter ten of the Classmate Murders and decided then to buy the next two books." ... "Just finished your third book, the Dominatrix Murders. I thought it was the best one of the three, didn't want to put it down till I finished it. I looked forward to see how Penny would greet (Jim) every day after her show. Keep the books coming can't wait for the next one."
A. Norris, retired Naval Corpsman

"If you like mysteries and action then don't miss reading this book..."
Jan Schneider, avid mystery/crime reader

"I've had the pleasure of meeting Bob Moats, he is the author of several "murder novels" with the first in the series being "The Classmate Murders". He gave me the opportunity to read "The Classmate Murders" which I found to be totally enjoyable. I must say the author weaves a wicked story plus his humor is a hoot! I shall not go into the plot because I don't want to ruin the read, but the novel will catch your interest within the first few pages. I recommend reading "The Classmate Murders"!

Doug Hardin, Author of "HIDDEN AND IMMINENT DANGERS"

Extra special thanks to:

Special thanks to Val Brooks who edited this book and for her great suggestions.

Re-edited March 2013

Thank you to all the people who purchased this book. I hope you enjoy it as much as I enjoyed writing it for my faithful readers.

The Jim Richards Family of Readers is listed in the back of the book.

Vegas Vigilante Murders
By Bob Moats

Chapter 1

The normal looking house on the far eastern edge of Las Vegas was dark that morning. A solitary light was burning in the hallway outside the bedrooms on the second floor, the light glowing into the open door of Jessica's room. The adorable ten-year-old child huddled on her bed while her father, Leo Meyer, beat her. Her whimpering and cries only made it worse as her father was even more enraged by her sobs causing him to assault her tiny little body harder.

"Shut up!" he screamed close up in her face as she tried to bite her lip to silence the sobs coming from her bruised throat where moments earlier he had nearly strangled her. "Shut the hell up or, so help me, I'll make you wish you were dead!"

"Maybe she isn't the one who should be dead," came a soft voice from behind Leo. He paused in his tirade on the girl and turned quickly to see a dark figure silhouetted in the doorway. The light from the hall shone brightly behind the man, his face darkened by the lack of light in the room. Leo reached over to turn on the small lamp resting on the child's bed stand to illuminate the stranger.

The person was dressed all in black clothing—black combat boots, black cargo pants and a black vest that made him look like he was part of a SWAT team. The man's face was hidden by a black mask reminding Leo of an executioner from medieval days.

"Who the hell are you?" Leo's words slurred from the over indulgence of alcohol he had consumed all night. "Get the hell out of here. This is my house. You have no business being here!"

The mystery man stepped backward into the hall and said softly, "Make me leave."

Leo stood the best he could and staggered towards the figure, more enraged than when he beat the girl. "I'll show you who will make you leave," he said, spitting out the words.

The figure turned from the door and was gone. Leo ran out and saw him standing by the stairs. Leo charged the man, but when he got to him, the dark figure grabbed Leo and with a vicious swing threw Leo down the stairs. Leo rolled and bumped downward until he came to a stop on the floor. The man came down the stairs and checked Leo. He was still moving. The stranger gave his head a sharp twist, snapping it in an unnatural direction.

He checked Leo's pulse. There was none. Seconds later the dark figure had vanished from the house.

The Las Vegas Metro 911 dispatcher answered the call and heard a small sobbing voice asking, "Please help me. I think my daddy is dead."

Vegas Vigilante Murders

~~*~~

The sun hadn't even risen yet, but already my darling Penny was having fits about what to wear for her talk show today. She was having three big name male hunks on her show promoting their movie filmed in Vegas. I sat on the edge of the bed as she flitted around the room pulling clothes from the closet over to Willy's chair. Willy, our ever-faithful toy Yorkie, was still on the chair trying to finish his sleep and didn't seem to be bothered by the ton of clothing piled on him.

I checked to see that he didn't suffocate, turned to my wife and said, "Why don't you just go on the show naked? I'm sure they would love that." My statement was followed by a shoe being thrown at my head as I retreated to the kitchen. I was trying to make some toast when Willy came flying in. I wasn't sure if he was alerted by my presence in the kitchen or chased out by Penny.

I was sitting at the snack bar munching my toast as Willy munched on his kibble when Penny came out wearing a short tight black dress with a string of pearls and long dangling earrings. Around her waist was a wide gold belt and she had matching gold high heels, spiked.

"Are you going out clubbing or hoping to entice one of your stars today?" I asked.

She stuck her tongue out and said, "I have to project an image of glamour for my viewers." She bent down to get a pan from the bottom drawer in the stove, riding her dress up and exposing her lace

8

underwear.

"The only thing you're going to project is those great black panties you're wearing." I smirked.

She quickly stood, realizing what she had done, looked at me for a moment and went back to the bedroom, whacking my arm as she passed.

She settled for a white silk blouse and a slightly longer skirt that wouldn't expose her to the lecherous panderings of her guests. I smiled at her as she stuck her tongue out again. She poured water in the pan and set the burner to heat the liquid. She then poured the oatmeal in as the water rolled and steamed.

"So what are you going to do today?" she asked me.

"I have a small case to find out if a wife is gambling the family savings away. Her husband can't quite seem to be able to follow her since she only goes out while he works, or so he thinks. I have to sit out front of the house and follow her to see if she is playing games of chance with their life savings."

"Sounds like fun. Don't get distracted by all the lovely women in the casinos."

"I keep my focus on the case, not the bevy of beauty found around the high rollers. Actually, most of the women in the casinos are ordinary wives or plain Jane types. The really good looking ones are in the private rooms for the big spenders, the whales."

"Well, remember the beauty you're married to. I don't want to ever find you chasing a skirt without a case behind it."

"Yes, dear. Oh, Buck picked up a new account for his guards yesterday. They will be guarding all the Gas-N-Go stations around Vegas. It should be very lucrative for the firm."

"How do you guys split up the money from all your ventures?"

"All income goes into one account and then we get a salary. It's all for bookkeeping and taxes, but we are investing in a bit in property, speculating on expansion of the casinos."

"You'll lose your shirts."

"Thanks for that nod of approval. Shouldn't you be going?"

She looked at the clock, wolfed down the rest of her oatmeal, grabbed her purse and briefcase, kissed my nose and headed out. I heard the garage door open and her car drove out the drive, setting off the driveway alarm. I went over and reset the thing then returned to my toast.

I dressed and got Willy ready for Lacey to pick him up and take him to our office. I had to go directly to the client's house to tail his wife so I wasn't going into the office right away. About ten minutes later the drive alarm went off again. It was Lacey. I reset the alarm again and then set the thing for twenty minutes to allow me time to leave.

The doorbell rang and I had Willy in his purse, his head sticking out of the opening, watching the door for Lacey. I opened the door, Willy yipped at Lacey, and she yipped back. I know she's a little childlike sometimes but I really believe she can communicate with Willy.

"Good morning, Lacey. How are you today?"

"I'm great. Mac got home around six this

morning from his guarding the car dealership and we had breakfast together. He said Buck may put him on the gas station detail, which would be nice. It's a day job so we can see each other more often," she bubbled.

"That's great. Nothing like passing each other going to your respective jobs."

"Yep, we now get about two hours together evenings and mornings. Not much time to do anything other than fool around." She blushed after she said that.

"I understand. Sex is a healthy part of a relationship." I smiled.

"Yes, but Mac doesn't like to rush, so our times together are spent fooling around and not getting much else accomplished." She blushed even redder.

"Okay, go before you start looking like a tomato." I laughed.

She thanked me, took Willy in his purse, and went off. I gathered up my camera case and a few other things I would need then went to the door just as my cell phone rang. It was Lynn. Usually when she called me early in the morning, it was police business and she wanted to ask me for advice. Although she and Deacon were talking about getting married, so I wondered if it could be about that.

"Hello, Dick Tracy. How are you this morning and what murder do you have for me to solve?" I said.

"You have a son so you may know more about children then I do. How do you get a kid to talk when she's frightened out of her skull?"

11

"Okay, start at the beginning."

"We got a 911 call this morning from a child saying her father was dead. When the first responders got there, they found him at the bottom of the stairs, dead, and the little girl was too frightened to talk. I would call child protective services, but I don't like those people. I have no experience with children and since you act like a child most the time, I thought you might help. Besides you're the grandfather type so she might relax around you."

"Thanks for the grandfather comment. I'll remember you in my will. I have a follow the wife case but I can put it off one more day. Where are you?"

"In my office. We brought her here and I think it frightened her even more."

I thought a moment and then said, "I have to swing by the office for something and I'll be in shortly." I hung up after she said she'd wait. I thought I might need a weapon to relax the child. I was going to pick up Willy.

**

Chapter 2

I breezed into my building lobby and found it empty but found Lacey in Trapper's office taking dictation. Trapper grinned when he saw me and said to Lacey that he would finish the letter later. I picked up Willy who was bouncing around my feet.

"Sending letters to your mom in Michigan?" I

asked with a smirk.

"Got to keep her informed of all the goings on here in her hometown. I'm hoping she may convince her husband to move back here so she's not so far away."

"I'd like it if my mother would move here, but she doesn't like the heat. She prefers the cooler Michigan weather. I hated the freezing cold in the winter and the damp humidity in the summer. At least here it's dry and fairly constant."

"I thought you had a case to go on this morning."

"I have to go to visit Lynn and Deacon. They have a small problem that needs my expertise. Are you doing anything for the next couple hours?"

"Nope, I'm free this morning. Whatcha got?"

I handed him a photograph and the address of the gambling wife. "I need to prove this woman, Alicia Barnes, is gambling away her food money. Her husband needs proof. Can you tail her and get some photos?"

"I can do that." He studied the photo, and I gave him the run down on when the husband left home for work. He said he'd take care of it. I went out to the lobby and stood looking at Lacey.

She was frowning wondering why I was looking at her. "What? Did I do something wrong?" she asked.

"No, I think I'll need you for a couple hours. Get your purse and Willy's purse and follow me." I went to tell Trapper to lock up the office when he left since Buck worked the night before filling in for a sick guard and wouldn't be in until later that day. I took

13

Lacey and Willy to the Crown Vic and drove over to Metro precinct.

We entered through the back entrance of the building and found Lynn and Deacon in her office just staring at the small girl sitting on a big chair in the corner of the room. Lynn saw us outside in the squad room and came out to talk to me.

"Thanks for coming. Hi, Lacey. Is she the reason you stopped at your office?"

"No, she was an afterthought. I went to get Willy. Lacey's young and maybe your girl will relax with her and Willy both."

Lynn smiled and explained what little they knew about the case then took us to her office. We entered the room and I saw a little girl looking shy and frightened sitting quietly in the corner. I asked Lynn and Deacon if they could leave us alone with her. They agreed and left.

I pulled up a chair and asked Lacey to sit then reached into the purse and took Willy out. I could see the girl's eyes growing at the sight of the pup, and she broke a small smile. I pulled over another chair and sat with Willy on my lap.

"Hi, Jessica. My name is Jim and this is Lacey. My little friend here is Willy. He is a teacup Yorkie, a small version of a Yorkshire terrier. Have you ever seen a dog this small?" I asked, hoping to get her to talk.

Her eyes were on Willy and she opened her mouth slightly then said quietly, "I never saw a dog like that."

"Would you like to hold him?" I asked.

She nodded her head and reached out. I carefully put him on her lap and she wrapped her arms around the pup. Willy was trying to lick Jessica's face and hands, causing the girl to laugh aloud.

The girl was adorable and had a face of a cherub, if I believed in cherubs. She had autumn brown hair and the bluest eyes I had ever seen on a child. It broke my heart to see the bruises on her neck and arms. How could any person be so cruel? We spent a few minutes letting Jessica play with Willy, and then I leaned forward and asked, "Jessica, may I ask you a few questions?"

She looked at me as Willy was lying on his back wanting attention from the girl. "What do you want to ask?"

"Well, can you tell me what happened this morning? We really need to know what happened. Why don't you tell Willy what happened?" I said, thinking maybe the dog might get better answers than I could.

She looked at Willy and said, "Hello, Willy. My dad was being mean to me. No one is mean to you, are they?"

"No, Willy is treated very well, Jessica. Can you tell him what happened to your father?"

She looked sad and I could see tears forming in her eyes. Lacey took a tissue from her purse and reached out to Jessica, giving her the tissue. "Take your time, Jess. May I call you Jess or do you like Jessica better?" I asked.

"I like Jessie. You can call me Jessie," she said quietly.

Vegas Vigilante Murders

"Okay, Jessie, that's a nice name. Now can you tell Willy what happened to your father?"

"My daddy was hitting me. He did that a lot. I tried to not cry but it hurt. He wouldn't stop. He was hitting me when this man came to the door of my bedroom. I couldn't see him. He was all black. He told my daddy that he should be dead and my daddy went after him. I couldn't see what happened in the hall but I heard a loud noise and waited to see if Daddy would come back. He didn't. I went to the hall and then to the stairs and I saw Daddy lying at the bottom. I went down and shook him but he didn't move. I knew to use the phone to call 911. They taught me that in school. I told the lady on the phone about my daddy and then sat until they came. They were all yelling and asking me loud questions. I was afraid."

"It's all right now, you're safe. What happened to the man in black?"

"I don't know. He was gone when I saw my daddy on the ground."

"Did your father hit you often?" I asked.

She nodded her head and looked down at Willy to avoid having to look back at us. "You couldn't see the face of the man at the door?" I asked.

"No, he had a black mask on. I didn't see his face. He was all black, his clothes and everything. Did he kill my daddy?"

"Well, we don't know that yet. It's what the police will find out, with your help," I said.

"I'm glad my daddy is dead. He beat my mommy and made her go away." She started crying. Lacey

16

went to her and hugged her, letting her cry on her shoulder. I went to the door after saying I'd be right back.

I went out and found Lynn and Deacon in the squad room listening to a monitor from a recorder attached to what I guessed was a wireless microphone in her office. "I didn't know your office was bugged," I said. She smiled and said it was something she set up for my questioning of the girl. "What happened to the girl's mother?" I asked.

"She's dead, under suspicious circumstances, died two months ago. They couldn't put it on the husband. He says he was with his lover that night, and the lover backs him up. They say she was killed during a home robbery, but I have my doubts." She looked through the window into her office, watching the girl petting Willy and not crying as hard. "That poor girl is an orphan now and will be taken away to be put in some foster home with people who don't give a rat's ass about her, just the money they'll make to take care of her."

"That sounds a little bitter. Do you have some experience with foster homes?" I asked.

"Yeah, too many years on the job taking depositions from abused and neglected children in foster homes. This town is built on gambling. Many of these foster home parents would use the money they get for taking care of the children and gamble it away. I don't have any love for foster care or Child Protective Services. They don't do a very good job of qualifying these people. That girl shouldn't be lost in the system. I've got Warren checking to see if there are any relatives in the area, but until then CPS will shuffle her around."

I was watching Lacey and Jessie playing with Willy and had an idea. I excused myself, went back into Lynn's office, and sat back in my chair. "Lacey, if I were to pay you to take care of Jessie for a while, would you be able to do that?"

Lacey look surprised and then turned to Jessie. "Would you like to stay with me and my boyfriend for a while? Until the police figure out what happened?"

Jessie looked at Willy and asked, "Would Willy be with us?"

"Well, Willy lives with me and my wife but you can visit with him often." I turned to the window. Lynn was smiling and gave me a thumbs up. I turned back to Jessie. "What school do you go to?"

"Martin Middle School, but I haven't been in school much. My daddy never let me go out much."

I thought probably because of the bruises on her which would raise a flag in school, bringing in CPS. I asked Lacey if there was a school near her home and she said there was one within walking distance. Now I had to convince CPS to allow Lacey and Mac to take care of her.

I excused myself again and went back to Lynn and Deacon. "Do you think I can pull it off?"

Lynn smiled and said, "I'll do my best to make sure it will happen."

**

Chapter 3

We were standing in the squad room watching Lacey and Jessie in Lynn's office when a rather portly woman with her mousy brown hair tied back in a tight bun stretching her face came up to us. "I'm looking for Lieutenant Carter."

Lynn gave the woman a suspicious eye and said, "That's me. Can I help you?"

"I'm Doris Braco from CPS. I was told by my supervisor that you had a child here in need of attention." The woman droned on like a recording.

"How did you find out so quickly?" Lynn asked.

"I was told that a policeman from a crime scene called. I went there but the child was taken here by you, I was informed," she said in the same monotonous kind of voice.

"Yes, we needed to ask her some questions about the incident at her home and with all the people going in and out of the crime scene and the ME removing her father, I felt it was better to have a quiet place to talk."

"I see. So will she be able to travel so we can place her in a youth home until a suitable arrangement can be made for her?"

I stepped forward and said, "Hi, Doris, my name is Jim Richards. I think we have a quick solution for the welfare of the child until the police can locate her relatives, which they are in the process of doing as I speak. So this may all be a moot point."

"I'm listening," she said.

"You see that woman in the office? She is my

personal assistant and she has agreed to watch the girl until we find her family. Would that be all right?"

"What is her status, her home life? Is she married?" the robot said.

"Well, she has a boyfriend she lives with, but they are engaged to be married. Her home is pleasant and there's a school quite close by."

"She's not married. They won't approve her," she said briskly.

I just stared at the woman, not liking her much. "So one would have to be married and have a good home environment to watch her until we find her family?" I kept mentioning the family aspect to be sure Doris knew that Jessie would be taken care of by her own people, hopefully soon.

"That's correct. If the young lady were married, it might be permissible."

"Well, I'm married and have a very good home, and there is a school bus that passes by my house every morning. I'd be willing to take her until such time as we find her relatives."

"I don't know you, Mr. Richards. Who are you?"

"I'm a private investigator, but you may know my wife, Penny Wickens."

Her eyes got a little life in them. Her tight lips were cracking a bit. "The talk show host of Vegas Alive. Yes, I know of her. You are married to her?"

"Yes, I am, and she only works about four hours a day. I could get the girl off to school in the morning. My hours are flexible. Then my wife would be home when she is dropped off. We have a dog as you can see," pointing to Willy, "and we have a stable environment in our home."

"I don't know, Mr. Richards. Could you at your advanced age take care of a child?"

I wasn't crazy about the advanced age comment but went on, "I raised a son I'm proud of and my wife adores children. This would just be until they find the child's family. Besides, your agency would have to pay to have her taken care of. I have a good deal of money to afford her anything that she would need and could save your budget a tidy sum." I think I hit a nerve. Her smile cracked slightly. I have found that money talks in this town.

"Yes, it would be a relief on our tight budget. The government is cutting back on things that shouldn't be messed with. The idiots they elect that don't know their elbows from a hole in the ground...sorry, it's a touchy subject to me. All right, Mr. Richards, you can take her but I will have to come by to check and see she is taken good care of."

"I whole heartedly agree. You can come by anytime. I'm sure you'd like to meet my lovely wife." Okay, I was spreading it on a bit thick but it was working.

"I'll need you to sign a few papers and it will be arranged." She turned to Lynn and asked if she could use a desk. Lynn guided her to the nearest empty desk in the squad room and Doris opened her satchel, took out some forms that she had me sign after filling in my address and phone number. She finished up and stood, shaking my hand. "So good of you, Mr. Richards. I'll look forward to meeting your wife." She turned on her heels and walked off.

"Now that was weird. They must thaw her out in the morning to do her job," Deacon said.

"Yep, but we are good to go now and saved one child from falling through the cracks. Do you think you can handle a child in your home, you know, as old as you are?" Lynn said.

"Why is everybody making comments about my age? I'm young at heart. That's what counts."

"Okay, grandpa, you should tell Jessie about her new move."

I stood looking at them, shook my head in resignation, and went into the office once more. I explained to Lacey about the marital problem. She was a little disappointed but said she'd like to help take care of Jessie whenever we needed it. I thanked her and sat. "Jessie, would you like to come stay with me and my wife for a while? Willy would be there for you to play with. Just until the police can find a relative that you can live with."

She nodded her head happily and asked if she could get some of her dolls and stuffed animals from her house to bring. I turned to Lynn through the opened door and asked if we could take her things from the house since it was a crime scene. Lynn said she and Deacon would go with us and help. I went back out to them and asked, "How did you know that it was a homicide, not just an accident of her father falling drunk down the stairs?"

"When the first responders arrived Jessie was sitting by the stairs and they asked her what happened. She was frightened but managed to say that some man hurt her father. That's when we were called in and the crime scene was secured."

"I see. Now I have to break the news to Penny that she's a mommy."

Lynn went in to bring Lacey and Jessie out of her office. Jessie was hanging on to Lacey and Willy for dear life, then when she got to me, she grabbed my hand and I could feel her squeeze it tightly.

"I don't think there is much more we will be able to get from her, so we may as well go get her things at the house. You can follow us," Lynn said.

We went out to our cars and drove over to Eastern and Sahara then into a small subdivision where we arrived at the house. There were still a couple police cars and a CSI SUV parked out front. Small groups of people were congregating out front watching, hoping to get a glimpse of something scandalous. Lynn and Deacon escorted us past the yellow tape barrier into the house, and then Lynn asked the lead CSI if they had the scene secured. He said we could take over, that they were finished.

I asked Jessie where her room was and she pointed up the stairway. Lacey was holding Willy in his purse and Jessie was hanging onto Lacey's arm. We went up and Lacey helped Jessie pack a good amount of clothing and toys to keep her for a while. I looked at the old and ratty clothes and could see that we would need to do some shopping for her. Penny would love that.

I looked around the room and asked Jessie if she could tell me what had happened that morning.

Jessie was silent for a moment and then said quietly, "I was on the bed and Daddy was standing here." She pointed. "Then the man came to the door. He said things to Daddy and then went down the hall. Daddy followed him and that's all I saw of the man."

Lynn spoke. "CSI found forced entry at the back of the house, but so far nothing to give us a clue as to who the mystery man was. He had to know the father and didn't approve of his actions towards the girl. That's all we have so far."

"Well, the father won't be brutalizing this child anymore," Deacon said.

We packed everything in my Crown Vic, and I thanked my friends and drove Lacey and Jessie to my office. We came in to find Trapper sitting at his desk printing out pictures of the gambling wife.

"That was fast," I said.

"Yep, as soon as hubby was out the door the wife was barreling down to the strip. She stopped at one of the smaller casinos, better odds there for the local folks to gamble. I got a good number of shots of her at the blackjack tables and roulette. She lost a small bundle before I left. I have enough photos to satisfy the husband."

"Thanks for that. Now come out to meet the newest addition to my family." He gave me a puzzled look and followed. He saw Jessie sitting on a chair next to Lacey's desk, holding Willy.

"Jessie, this is my friend and business partner, Will Trapper. He used to be a police detective in Detroit." Jessie smiled and waved to him. He waved back.

Trapper turned to me and quietly asked, "Does Penny know about this?"

I laughed and explained the whole story to him. He was watching Jessie as I finished. "Poor kid, not a good life." As he said that, the front door opened and in walked Penny.

"Hey, babe, come on over and meet your new daughter."

She gave me a look and then saw Jessie. She smiled and asked, "Where did you kidnap her from and is she worth a lot?"

**

Chapter 4

I called Jessie over and she brought Willy with her. "Penny, this is Jessie Meyer." Penny said hello as I knelt down and said to her, "Jessie, this is my wife, Penny Wickens. She has a talk show on TV in the mornings. Maybe someday you can go with us to see a show being taped. Would you like that?" She nodded her head. I said to go back to Lacey while I talked to Penny. We went into my office for privacy and I explained my morning to her.

She smiled when I finished. "You just love bringing home stray women, don't you? First Lacey now Jessie. As long as they're too young for you, it's okay by me. So what's this I heard you mention about needing to shop for clothes?"

"Yep, her clothes are pretty sad looking. I watched as she packed. I figured you'd like to take her shopping for a new wardrobe."

"Is the sky blue? Of course I'll take her shopping.

Do you need her right now?"

"Nope, she's just here because I was bringing Lacey back to work then you showed up. So go have fun. I'm sure Jessie will love the outing. Her father didn't let her out of the house much." I stood, went to the door and called Jessie in. She came in with Willy, and I asked her to sit. "Jessie, Penny is going to take you shopping for new clothes. How does that sound?"

Her eyes went wide and she gave me a big grin, nodding her head.

Penny reached over and petted Willy. "I see Willy has a new friend now. So you are going to be staying with us for a while. Do you swim?"

I knew Penny would get around to the pool question. Jessie opened her mouth and said, "I never learned to swim."

"Well, we have a real big pool and I'm going to teach you to swim. Willy knows how to swim so you and he can swim together."

Jessie looked at Willy and smiled.

I said, "You better pick up some water wings or a life jacket until she gets proficient at swimming."

Penny stood and told Jessie to go out to the other room and they would leave. She looked at me and said, "Do you need Lacey? I'd like to take her to help with our shopping."

"No, go and have fun. Do you need any cash?"

"I always need cash but I have enough to handle the situation. Thanks." She went out as I followed her.

Lacey was at her desk putting make-up on Jessie.

She smiled and said, "Can't send a woman out into the public without a little make-up, now can we?"

I figured Lacey was trying to cover up the bruises on Jessie's neck, which was good of her. Lacey finished the cover up make-up with a hint of eye shadow and light lipstick. Jessie looked quite cute for a nine year old. She looked at herself in Lacey's hand mirror and got a huge smile on her face. Penny asked Lacey if she'd like to go with her to help shop for clothes for Jessie. She asked me if she could leave work. I said there wasn't a whole lot going on so she could go. They gathered themselves up and left.

I sat with Trapper in his office talking for a while then Buck came in. "Hey guys, what's happening?"

"Not much. I had a murder case come in this morning, but I ended up with a nine year old girl to take care of," I said with a big smile. Buck gave me a puzzled look so I explained the whole story to him.

"Wow. Do you think you can handle a child running around your home? You might hurt your old body," he said with a grin.

"Why is everyone getting on me about my age? I'm actually a thirty year old in a mature body. So leave it at that!"

Buck winked at Trapper and went to his office. My cell phone rang and Penny said she was dropping off Lacey then heading home so she asked me to pick up a pizza or some other good food. I said I would and hung up.

A few minutes later the front door opened and it was Lacey. She came back and said, "Wow, did we get clothing for Jessie! It took two shopping carts to haul it to the car."

I smiled and said, "It's late so go home to see Mac off to work."

I could hear Buck yell from his office, "Mac isn't working tonight. I'm starting him on the gas stations tomorrow morning."

Lacey made a silent whoop and gave me a big smile as she left. I went to Buck's door and said, "You just made a young girl very happy."

About an hour later I arrived at the house with two big pizza boxes and went in to find Penny and Jessie with clothing all over the living room. I couldn't believe how many items they had. Jessie was bouncing all over the place holding clothes up and then she would disappear into the guestroom to change.

"I hope you left some clothing for the other little girls," I said as I kissed Penny hard on the lips.

"Well, that was nice. Are you expecting something in return? You know we have to be discreet with a child around the house."

I hadn't thought about that little fact. Even though our bedrooms weren't that close, we could get loud sometimes, especially Penny. "Well, we'll just have to improvise. Besides, we can go out to the guest house."

We ate our pizza, had our refreshments, and watched a little television. Jessie was on the floor playing with Willy, and we looked like a happy family.

Later Penny tucked Jessie into bed and came

back to me in our bedroom. "She went right to sleep as I was folding her clothes for her. She's a quick sleeper."

I grabbed onto her and pulled her on the bed with me, kissing her hard and long.

"Watch that buster. It could lead to things you may not be able to handle." She gave me her evil little smile.

I just said, "Try me."

Willy was missing from his chair as I went to the bathroom after we quietly made love. Penny said he wouldn't leave Jessie's room. "I guess we know where his loyalties are." I finished my business and got back into bed.

"See, we can still fool around as long as you don't yell a lot," I joked. About a half hour later we were both asleep.

It was four in the morning when I heard the screams. Penny was out of bed before I even sat up. She was heading to Jessie's room. I threw on a robe and followed. Jessie was sitting up in bed crying as Penny held her. She looked at me and said, "She had a bad dream about...well, you know what."

I had a feeling this would be hard on Jessie with all the abuse and then seeing her father dead. It might take a little professional help for her. I would call Lynn and ask if she knew anyone, but I would call later. Penny sat with Jessie for a while longer. They were talking and I went out to the kitchen to get a glass of water for Jessie.

We were all back in bed by five and I nodded off quickly for once.

Vegas Vigilante Murders

~~*~~

Hector Ramirez had just returned from the bar he frequented and was staggering through the apartment looking for his wife who was hiding in the bathroom. He banged on the door loudly and screamed for her to open up. He had a Bowie knife in his hand and was driving the point into the door, just stabbing and stabbing at the wood, leaving deep cuts in the veneer.

"Open this damn door, Celeste! Open it or I swear to God I'll break it down!" He started pounding harder and the thin-skinned door started to crack in the middle. He managed to break an opening in the door as the wood gave way. He peeked in and gave a grin, paraphrasing the line from The Shining, "Here's Hector." Celeste watched in terror as he reached in to unlock the bathroom door.

As he was reaching down, Celeste saw a black gloved hand come around his mouth and he was yanked back from the door. Celeste sat on the floor in wonder as to what just happened. She carefully got up, went to the door and heard a struggling noise and muted screams. She looked through the opening and saw a black clad figure strangling Hector with his hands. Hector's eyes were bugging out and his tongue was sliding in and out of his mouth. After a moment, Hector gave up the struggle and went limp. The figure dropped him and turned to look at the opening in the door. Celeste took a deep breath as she saw that the man had on a black mask. He saluted her then disappeared down the hallway. She looked down at the lifeless body of Hector, afraid to come out of the bathroom until she felt safe.

She waited about fifteen minutes, listening for any sign that someone was in the apartment. She went to the door, unlocked it and came out slowly, seeing Hector still on the floor. She went to the phone and dialed 911.

Being Mexican, she mustered up her best English and said, "I need police. Someone has murdered my husband."

**

Chapter 5

Deacon arrived at the crime scene about twenty minutes after Warren called him. Warren had determined that this murder possibly had something to do with the Meyer murder yesterday morning. Both victims had been abusers of either women or children and were killed by a dark-dressed man.

"Hey, Greg, whatcha got?" Deacon asked as he entered the apartment.

"Same MO as your vic yesterday. Hector Ramirez abused his wife. We had numerous calls to this address previously when he would kick the crap out of her, but she would never prosecute. Looks like someone decided to do it for her. So far it's shaping up to be a vigilante. At least it looks that way to me." He bent down, pointing to the bruises on Ramirez's neck where he was strangled. "The perp had to be strong to do this to his beefy neck. Joe Lang told me after he examined the body that the vic had enough muscle to fight off the attacker, but evidently couldn't."

Joseph Lang, Clark County-Las Vegas medical examiner, walked up as they were looking at the body. "Where's your partner, Deacon?"

"Lynn got called into the captain's weekly meeting. You know crime has to stop when the captain needs to let everyone know how we're doing in fighting crime. Our closure rate is up, which is good, but the captain wants it closer to a hundred percent rather than seventy-six. Lynn hates the meetings but has to be there."

"When are you going to make an honest woman out of her?" the ME asked.

"We've been talking about marriage, but if we do they may separate us. I might get a new partner like Warren. I dread that." Warren gave Deacon the middle finger. "So far we've been discreet about living together. The captain is so scattered I don't think he knows. But Lynn has been having wedding blues lately so it may happen soon. What's the word on the vic, Joe?"

"Well, as Warren already filled you in, he was strangled. The vic had a thick neck, mostly fat, so the perp would have had good strong hands to squeeze his windpipe shut. Ramirez weighed in about 280 to 300 and was built for construction, which he did for a living, so he could have fought off his attacker. The alcohol probably slowed him down. He was stinking drunk as you probably can smell."

Deacon was examining the bathroom door as the

ME was talking. He was running the scene through his head, visualizing what might have happened. Warren came up to him and said, "We were able to talk to the wife through a translator. She's pretty new from Mexico. Hector brought her up about six months ago, illegally of course, but married her in a quickie Vegas wedding ceremony, so she's good to stay here. She says Hector came in from his favorite bar and she heard him yelling before he even got into the apartment. She didn't want to be beaten again, so she locked herself in the bathroom. He broke through the door as you can see, but as he was trying to unlock the door a hand grabbed him from behind and pulled him away. She went to the door and saw a man dressed all in black killing her husband. Whoever it was left in a hurry. That's all she said."

"You may be right, Greg, could be the beginnings of a vigilante, and I have a feeling there'll be more. This town is full of frustrated, mean people who need to be taken down a peg." Deacon smiled as he looked down at the vic.

"You're not condoning murder, are you, Deacon?" Warren asked.

"No, that's illegal and immoral, but sometimes I root for the good guy to win once in a while. I suppose CSI didn't turn up anything?"

"Nope, nothing definite so far but they won't know till they get everything back to the lab."

Deacon's cell phone went off and he saw by the caller ID that it was Lynn. He answered and heard her say, "You won't believe what the captain is making me do!"

Vegas Vigilante Murders

~~*~~

It was Thursday morning so I told Penny that we could wait until Monday to take Jessie to register for school. "Give her a few days to relax before throwing her to the wolves. She can visit with Lacey and Willy at the office or go in and annoy Buck for a while. He's not crazy about children."

"Just don't teach her any bad habits and keep her away from Trapper. He'll have her pulling pranks on everyone." Penny smiled as she got ready to go to her studio to do her show. "I have some knights and kings from the Excalibur Hotel show coming in tomorrow. I'll take Jessie with me. She may get a kick out of the horses they'll be bringing."

"Sounds good," I said as Jessie entered the kitchen where Penny was making a big pot of oatmeal. She made extra for Jessie and set two bowls on the snack counter. I helped Jessie get up on the stool as she said good morning. She dug into the oatmeal as if she was starved.

"My father didn't cook and I wasn't very good at it, so I usually ate dry cereal in the mornings. This is good, thank you." Jessie and Penny both wolfed down the food after Penny sprinkled a little cinnamon on their oatmeal. I was holding in a laugh watching the two of them. They looked so much alike.

Penny went off to work and I gathered Willy in his purse which Jessie asked if she could carry. I let her. We drove over to the office and went in to find Lacey already at her desk.

"Good morning to both of you." She beamed.

"So did you enjoy having Mac around the house last night?" I asked.

"Yes, it was very nice and we got a lot accomplished." She started to blush again.

"Okay, take a breath and relax. I've never seen a person turn red as fast as you do. You can baby sit Willy and Jessie for the day. I have a client coming in to discuss a case with me."

Jessie spoke up. "I don't need a babysitter. I'm nine and I have been taking care of myself for a while. My father never spent much time around the house." She choked up a little so I changed the subject.

"Lacey, why don't you tell Jessie about what we do here, the investigating and security. Tell her all about how we met you and the crime we solved. Just don't be too graphic." I smiled and went to see if Trapper was in. He was.

"Nothing better to do around Vegas than sit in your office?" I asked.

He looked up from what he was writing. "I'm making my report for your client about his wife's gambling excursion yesterday. I thought when I left the police I wouldn't have to do reports again. Oh well."

"I think the paperwork here is going to be a lot less than you had back at your old precinct," I said. I heard the front door bell tinkle and looked out to see Lynn come storming down the hall followed by Deacon.

"Son-of-a..." she started to yell, but paused

looking around. "Where's the kid?"

"You passed her in the lobby. What's got your back up?" I asked.

"The captain wants to send me to FBI training for law enforcement officers at the FBI Academy in Quantico, Virginia! They take police in to train them in various things like terrorism and kidnapping and whatever else the FBI does. I have to go for a month. Do you believe that?!" I could almost see steam coming from her ears.

"It may be good for you to get away from all of us nuts here," I said. "Change of scenery."

"I don't like scenery, I don't like change! I don't want to go!" Deacon came up and started rubbing her shoulders. Her eyes rolled back and she gave a big sigh. "Oh, keep that up. I needed to get the tension out."

"When do you go?" I asked.

"Tomorrow morning. Do you believe that? Not even a couple days to get ready. They have a new class registration starting late tomorrow and the captain didn't think to schedule it earlier," she moaned.

Deacon guided her to Trapper's client chair and pushed her to sit as he turned to me. "We got another abuse killing this morning."

"And?"

"It was similar to the murder of Jessie's father, an abuser who beat on his wife killed by a man in black. Warren says he thinks it's a vigilante."

"See, I'm needed here, not in Quantico," Lynn said from her chair.

"Go have fun, I can handle it." Deacon was probably glad that he could take lead for once on a case. Lynn was always in the front of everything. Deacon was the guy in the rear.

"I know you can handle it. I just hate to be out of the loop. I need to go home to pack. Let's get out of here. Say so long to Penny for me."

"You're only going to be gone for a month. You'll be back," I offered.

Deacon smiled and said to me, "I'll keep you informed about this vigilante. Maybe Jessie can remember something that might help." He helped Lynn out of her chair and they went out of Trapper's office. Trapper and I followed them to the lobby where they said their hellos and good-byes to Lacey and Jessie and went out.

I saw a car pulling into a parking space out front as Deacon drove off. It was my gambling wife client. I warned Trapper and he went back to his office. I said I'd bring him back there to discuss his wife. The man entered the front door and I greeted him. "Good morning, Mr. Barnes. I have some information to give you if you'll just follow me." We went back to Will's office and Trapper stood and asked him to sit.

"Will, this is Chester Barnes. Mr. Barnes, this is Will Trapper, my associate. He followed your wife yesterday. He has everything you requested as to your wife's activities," I said.

Trapper took out the folder he had prepared and opened it, placing it in front of Barnes. He said, "After you left for work yesterday, your wife was out of the house and drove first to the Terrible's Hotel and Casino where she proceeded to gamble away about two thousand dollars. She then proceeded to the Silver Dollar Casino and lost another thousand. I stopped following her there since I had all the evidence that you requested."

**

Chapter 6

Barnes leaned to the desk to study the pictures closer. He frowned and said, "I don't know where Alicia's getting the money. Her bank account is almost drained, but you say she dropped almost three thousand dollars that you witnessed. She doesn't have that kind of cash. How could she be doing this?"

"Well, we found out about her gambling. How she found the funds is another matter," I said.

"I'd like to retain you to investigate how she could be affording to drop this kind of money. Can you do that?"

I looked at Trapper and he nodded. "I think we can help you or at least try to find out about your wife's activities. I'll let Trapper get some information from you about your wife's financials and anything else he will need to proceed if that is all right with you."

"Of course. I need to know where the money is coming from before I confront her about the gambling. If there is anything illegal, I need to know."

"We'll do our best to find out as quickly and

quietly as possible," Trapper offered.

Barnes took out his checkbook and said he was writing the retainer fee as we had agreed on when he first came to request my help. He handed me the check and I put it in my jacket pocket. "We'll get on this as soon as possible. I'll leave you two to work out the details." I thanked him and went out to the lobby to give Lacey the check to deposit. I looked into Buck's office but he wasn't in. I figured he was out getting the gas stations set up for his guards.

I was standing in the lobby ruminating on how busy this morning was becoming and thinking about Lynn going off to train with the FBI. I remembered back in Michigan when there was a flap about sending a couple of cops from a local precinct to train. The city said it didn't have the budget to pay for the training, but they yielded and sent just one of the officers.

Barnes came out of the hallway followed by Trapper. They shook hands and then Barnes shook mine, thanked us and left. "He gave me a number of leads I can check on, but I'll have to follow the wife more now. I'll start in the morning since I have no idea where she is right now. Barnes works as a manager at an Albertson's grocery, so he has long hours, giving the wife plenty of time to wander. I hope she wanders in the right directions." He headed back to his office.

I was watching Jessie playing with Willy by Lacey's desk thinking about her dead father and the new murder this morning of another abuser. Could this be a serial vigilante or just two connected murders of people someone didn't like? I guessed if there were any more, we would know. I went into my office to look busy and wait for something else to happen.

About an hour later Penny came into the building and stopped to say hi to Lacey and Jessie. Willy ran around the counter and bounced at her feet. "Oh, now you want attention after you ignored me this morning," she said to the dog. She picked him up and nuzzled him as I came out of the office.

"Can I get a little of that too?" I asked.

She held out the dog and said, "Sure go ahead and hug him too."

"I meant hugging you." I smiled and gave her a kiss. "How was your show?"

She looked at the TV in the lobby. "Don't you people ever watch me?"

"We've been busy. But I'll make sure Lacey turns it on from now on." I laughed. "Oh and Lynn is leaving us for a month to go train with the FBI in Quantico. She's going to come back a super spy."

"Wow, can I go too?"

"If you want, but you'll have to pay your own way."

"I can afford it. Will there be any good looking Feebies?"

"Don't say that in front of Deacon. He'll fret about her till he ends up flying out there."

Penny turned to Jessie and said, "Jessie, you're going with me tomorrow morning to watch me tape my show. We're going to have knights in shining armor and horses. How's that sound?"

Jessie's eye grew and she broke out in a big grin. "I'd love that!"

I saw that Lacey was looking excited too and I asked Penny, "Would it be all right if Lacey went too?"

"Sure, she and Jessie can sit together while I do the show." That was my point, Lacey could watch Jessie so she'd be safe. I think Penny caught that.

Lacey was as excited as Jessie and I told her to be at our home early. She agreed. I took Penny in my office and we sat.

"Deacon had another case this morning. A man who habitually abused his wife was murdered by a man in black."

"Hmm, sounds familiar. You haven't said anything to Jessie?"

"No, I don't feel that bit of info needs to be relayed to her. I'm trying to keep the subject of her father to a minimum."

"They have any leads so far?"

"Not that Deacon told me. I think he is a little happy that Lynn is going to be gone. He can run a case by himself now."

"Ah, a little jealousy on his part that he's always the second banana."

"Yeah, something like that. Deacon is a good cop and was very helpful back when we ran together solving crimes. I know he can handle it."

Trapper came to my office door and said hi to Penny. "I'm going out to see a few friends in law enforcement to get some info on my client's wife."

I smiled and said, "Gee, the shoe is on the other

41

foot now. You the P.I. calling in favors from the cops. Sound familiar?"

"Yes, and you were a pain in the butt, always asking for information, but I enjoyed it. I'll be back later." He said his good-byes and left.

Penny spoke. "How's it going working with Will?"

"It's been good. I like having him here to do the leg work and he loves it."

Buck came in through the back door and stopped by my office.

"Hell man, this gas station gig is going to be rough," he said.

"Why?"

"You should see all the nut cases coming in for gas, supplies, beer and cigarettes. Up at the north end stations I saw enough lower class people looking suspicious as if they could rob the place. I don't know why they don't install those Plexiglas booths around the cashier. It would be a lot safer. I got all my guards armed in these stations. They'll need it."

"I hope no one gets hurt. Where did you put Mac?"

"I got him patrolling the stations, checking on the guards, sort of as a supervisor. That should keep him safe, and Lacey won't shoot me if he gets hurt." Buck gave his big walrus smile and excused himself to go to his office.

Nothing much was going on up to five o'clock, so I turned Lacey loose to go see Mac then gathered up our stuff to go home. "Buck, we're taking off. You staying?"

"Yep, Maria has an early show tonight. The Tropicana expects their dancers to be there so she'll be gone most the night. I'll just sit here working on the schedule for the stations."

"Okay, we'll see you tomorrow." I left him to his business and took my girls out to the Crown Vic. "Anyone feel like Sonic burgers and onion rings?" I asked. That met with an enthusiastic response, so I drove over and we had our meal.

Back at home, we relaxed and I put on a Wii game of bowling I bought a couple months back to play when friends came over. Penny and Jessie were having a ball with it as I went to work on my next book in my home office. Around seven I looked out my back window to the pool and saw Penny and Jessie in swimsuits as Penny was explaining the finer points of swimming to Jessie. They spent about an hour getting Jessie used to the water and then they came back in the house. Penny came to my room and said, "She'll do fine in the water, just a few more lessons." Then she went off. Around ten, we decided to head to bed.

"Are you two going to be making noise again tonight?" Jessie asked.

"What do you mean?" Penny asked but figured she knew to what Jessie was referring.

"Last night I got up to get a drink of water and could hear you in your room making funny noises."

I looked at Penny with a smile. "We were goofing around, that's all. Just play acting."

"Oh, I thought you were having sex," she said casually.

Vegas Vigilante Murders

Penny got big eyed and whispered to me, "We'll have to leave a bottle of water in her room from now on."

~~*~~

Four-thirty in the morning was a time for children to be asleep in bed, but not so for six year old Noel Hendricks. Her father, Murphy, was in her room doing things to her that no father should be doing. She was on the bed, not moving for she knew if she did, it would result in a beating. The father was about to slip her pajama gown up when he heard a knocking noise, like someone tapping on the wall outside of the room. He stood and went to the door slowly. When he reached the door it flew open and there stood a man all in black. He reached out to Murphy and grabbed him by the shirt, pulling him out of the room. Noel heard muffled screams and a banging noise. It was from Murphy Hendricks' arms and legs flailing around, hitting the walls as the man in black was hoisting him up by his neck, hanging him.

Murphy ceased moving when his neck snapped, and the man dropped him. He then undid Murphy's belt and pulled down his pants. The man pulled out a knife, castrated the dead man, and stuffed the parts into his mouth. Noel was watching from her bedroom door as the man looked up at her, putting his finger to his masked mouth, signaling her for silence. Then he turned and went out of the hallway and out of the house.

44

Noel went to her mother's room where the woman hid when her husband was doing things he shouldn't but she was too afraid to stop him. Noel knocked on her mother's door and when the woman asked what she wanted, Noel just said quietly, "I think Daddy's sleeping."

**

Chapter 7

Penny and Jessie were up early getting ready to go to her station to tape the show of knights and kings. Lacey showed up and they all piled into Penny's car and drove off, Lacey taking charge of Willy, leaving me all alone. It was nice and quiet in the house when I heard the driveway alarm go off. "Crap, did they forget something?" I wondered and went to the security panel to turn on the monitor. I saw Deacon in the driveway getting out of his car. I went to the front door and opened it, allowing him to enter.

"Did you get Lynn off this morning?" I asked then realized what I had said.

Deacon grinned and said, "Yes, I did, then I took her to the airport. She is winging her way to Virginia as we speak, and I got another abuse killing." He came into the kitchen following me as I was putting two pieces of bread in the toaster.

"Okay, this is three kills in three days. What happened this time?" I asked.

"A father who was sexually abusing his daughter

got it really good. He had his balls stuffed into his mouth, although it was after he was hung up and had his neck snapped. Should have been done before he died to let him know how it feels to be raped." Deacon sounded mad.

"I empathize with you. I don't care much for these scum who abuse helpless women and children. Was the child taken by CPS?" I asked.

"No, this one had a mother. She would look the other way when her husband would do his dirty business. The child watched the man kill her father, and she didn't care. Amazing, she was six years old and knew that her father was never going to hurt her again. I think she is going to need years of therapy." Deacon just stared at the walls. "I'm supposed to catch this guy, but I feel he is doing a justice to these victims of abuse. I'm a cop and have to stand by my oath of supporting the law, but times like these try my faith. We have no way to protect his potential victims if we don't know who they are. We have a huge list of reported abusers, so how do we find this guy's victims out of a couple thousand scums?"

"Was there any connection between the victims?"

"None that I know of yet. I could use an extra eye on the case if you have the time."

"I don't have anything scheduled. Trapper is taking a case I was supposed to do, so it freed me up. Penny took Jessie, Willy and Lacey into her station for her show, so I'm alone today. What would you like me to do?"

"Just tail along and if you see something I miss,

give me a heads up."

"I can do that. Just say the word to go."

"Okay, go." He grinned and we got ready to leave. I set the alarms and we went out to his car after I left a note on the snack bar that I was with Deacon in case Penny came home instead of going to the office. I called Buck from the car and told him I would be out all morning and Lacey was with Penny. He said he had nothing to do but paperwork, so he'd hold down the office.

Deacon drove us to the home of the latest murder. There were still a couple patrol cars and a CSI SUV in front. There were also about ten reporters and their vans congregating on the front lawn just outside of the yellow tape. We went in and the cop on duty was glad to see Deacon. "I've been flooded with these damn reporters trying to get in and bothering the CSI techs."

"You have my permission to shoot them," Deacon joked. The cop smiled and said the mother was in the living room. We went in and found the woman sitting on a couch with her daughter lying next to her with her head on her mother's lap. The girl had her eyes closed. I didn't know if she was sleeping or just not wanting to watch.

Deacon sat on an easy chair across from the woman. Her daughter opened her eyes. She had almost grey pupils like a wolf. It was startling.

"Mrs. Hendricks, I'm Detective DeAngelo and this is Jim Richards, a civilian advisor to the police. I know this is difficult and I'm sorry but I have to ask you and your daughter some questions. May I?"

"I hope this man gets away with this. Murphy was a rotten evil person and he deserved to die. Now I have to reverse a couple years of torture that my daughter went through."

"I understand, and I sympathize with you, but if you can tell me anything about this morning, that might help."

"I didn't see any of it. I was in my room hiding like I always did. I'm gutless and I admit it. I should have been the one to cut his balls off." Tears were coming to her eyes. She had a tissue and used it.

"Mrs. Hendricks, did your daughter tell you anything about the man?"

"She said he was all black. I presume she meant his clothing. He came in the door as my husband heard a noise and went to see what it was. The man grabbed my husband and Noel said he made him sleep. That's all, other than she came to my door to let me know. I came out, found him in the hall, and asked Noel what happened. That's when she told me. I immediately called the police to report it. I wasn't sure if the killer was still in the area."

"Thank you, ma'am. Jim, do you have any questions?"

I sat on the arm of the chair Deacon was sitting in and asked, "Did you ever report your husband's activities with your daughter?"

"Oh God, no, he would have killed me."

"Did you tell anyone else about the abuse? A friend maybe?"

"No, I didn't tell anyone. But one time a doctor was asking about bruising on her body when I took her for a booster shot. I lied through my teeth to get out of there before he called Child Protective Services. Maybe I should have let them. It would have saved her from further grief at the hands of that bastard."

Deacon asked what doctor she took the child to.

"It was at the mission clinic up by Fremont Street. We don't have health insurance, thanks to the Republicans, or much money, so we went there. I don't remember the name of the doctor. I can give you the address."

"That would be great, ma'am," Deacon said. She moved Noel off her lap and went to get the address then wrote it down for Deacon.

Deacon stood and thanked her. "We may have more questions later, but for now, we'll leave you alone."

She walked us to the door and we went out. "I think you should ask the Mexican woman what clinic she goes to," I said.

Deacon pulled his cell phone and called Warren to ask him if he could get the translator back to the Ramirez woman to see if she went to the 6th Street Mission clinic. He said he would and Deacon hung up. "Could be a connection. See if Jessie ever went there also."

I said I'd check later and we went to Deacon's car. We sat there for a moment and I said to wait. I pulled my cell phone and called Lacey. She came on and I said, "Are you close to Jessie?" She said she was next to her. I asked her to ask Jessie if she ever went to a doctor's office up on 6th Street in a mission.

Vegas Vigilante Murders

I heard her asking and they talked a minute then Lacey came back on. "Yep, she says she went there for a sprained wrist. Her mother took her a couple months ago, just before she went away." I thanked her and said I thought we might have a connection.

We drove up to 6th Street, found the mission church, and parked out front. We found a sign pointing out where the free clinic was around the side. We went in and found it filled with women and children. There must have been twenty to thirty people crammed into the small lobby. Deacon went to the desk, pulled his badge, and asked for someone in charge. The receptionist look frazzled, picked up the phone and made a brief call. She said the doctor would be out in a moment. We stood looking at the sea of poor people waiting for help for themselves or their children. I felt really bad that they had to resort to low quality health care, although I was sure that the people in charge made it as respectable as possible for them.

About ten minutes later an older woman in a lab coat came out. "I'm Doctor Lorraine Wilson. What's your business here for wasting my time?"

Deacon said, "I'm sorry to hold you up but we've had three murders of men who have abused a woman and two children who may have been treated here. It's our only lead for right now."

"Is this the murders they have been running on the television all morning?" she asked.

"I haven't been watching the TV but I'm sure it is. Can you help us?"

"I can't give out any information about our

patients. If you get a warrant I would be forced to help you."

"Do the names Celeste Ramirez, Jessica Meyers or Noel Hendricks mean anything?" I asked.

The doctor looked slightly unsettled by the question, but said, "No, and I can't give out any information. Get a warrant and come back." She turned and went back into the door she came out of.

I turned to Deacon and said, "That went well, wouldn't you say?"

**

Chapter 8

Trapper was resting his feet on the desk of a friend from back in the days when Trapper was a rookie cop on the bike police patrolling the Vegas strip.

"Are you comfortable?" Detective Josh Harper asked Trapper as he came back into the cubicle that he called his office. Trapper took his feet down and laughed, saying, "I was just getting there."

"So did you get anything on the wife and her husband?" Trapper asked, leaning forward as Harper sat.

"Well, Barnes doesn't have much of a sheet, and I couldn't find a dent in his financials. He's squeaky clean. Employer says he's a good worker, manages an Albertson's and has no tickets. Retired from 20 years in the Army as a captain in intelligence and served two tours in Nam. Now Alicia Barnes is another story. She has a number of speeding tickets, probably from rushing to get to the casinos, and her financials are a little strained. I was able to quietly pull her records, and her funds have been up and down but mostly down. There's nothing I can see that shows she could afford to drop three hundred dollars, let alone three thousand dollars. If she is betting like this every morning, either she'd have to be printing the cash or has a very big bag of money stashed away. I did find one reference for her being pulled in for soliciting in the Golden Nugget hotel, but charges were dropped and it was swept under the rug. Someone was on her side or had money. Maybe she's hooking on the side in other hotels for her gambling money."

Trapper thought about that. He knew he had a few connections to find out if she was a working girl or just a loose housewife. "Thanks, Josh, I appreciate the help. You know that you're my bitch now." He laughed.

"Don't push your luck. I'm in a generous mood today. Now get out of my office so I can get back to real crimes."

Trapper stood, shook his hand and walked out of the cubicle, nearly walking into Captain Weber. Luckily, Weber was walking and reading from a folder at the same time and didn't notice Trapper so Will went out quickly. Not that he was trying to avoid Weber, but he would end up having to listen to him talk for about an hour of precious time. Trapper went to his car and sat gathering his thoughts.

Trapper pulled his cell phone and called me.

When I answered he said, "Hey, Alicia Barnes is destitute but can drop thousands of dollars in casinos all over town. I smell crime here. How you doing?"

I quickly explained my morning and then said, "Deacon and I are at the 6th Street Mission Clinic not getting any cooperation from the doc in charge, of course, but Deacon has called in for a warrant so we can go through the files of our victim's family since they may have dealt here. It's a connection."

"Good one too. Think about it. The people at the clinic know who comes in with a hint of abuse, and someone in the place is using that knowledge to avenge these folks. A doctor or orderly, if they have any orderlies. Hell, it could even be a strong nurse."

"Yep, you're on the beam, but we only have the word of two abused people that came here. We are waiting for word from the third if she was a patient. Then we'll have a tight connection."

"Okay, I'm going to track down my gambling housewife and follow her the rest of the day. She may lead me to a higher crime, which would be nice."

"You really want this to turn into a major deal, don't you? Following a wife is not just enough for you, is it?"

"I got to have a good murder or extortion or something really meaty or I'm not happy."

"Well, good luck. Deacon's phone just rang. It may be some good news. Talk later." I hung up and turned to Deacon.

He was listening to someone and then hung up. "Celeste Ramirez told the translator that she came to this clinic without her husband's knowledge to have an infection treated. She figures her husband brought it home from his fooling around. The people in the clinic were real curious about her bruises but she brushed them off by pretending she didn't understand them." He got on his cell phone again and called Warren to tell him to push the warrant through. We had all three vics' families tied to the clinic. He hung up, looked at me, and said, "Now we just wait."

Doctor Lorraine Wilson was not pleased when we came back with Warren and two patrol officers. Deacon presented the warrant that Warren delivered to the doc and politely asked if we could see their file system.

The doctor said to a nurse briskly, "Take these policemen to the patient file cabinets and let them search. But make sure they do not mess up the files. Watch them closely." She turned to us and continued, "I have patients to care for so, if you'll excuse me." She turned and walked away leaving us with the nurse, a rather attractive young brunette with a great smile.

She was making eyes at Deacon who was trying to keep his composure. I was smiling, remembering when I first met Deacon and he was getting the eye from one of Penny's make-up girls at her studio back in Michigan. He cleared his throat and asked the nurse, "If you could take us there now."

She led us to a room that had about ten tall, wide file cabinets lining the walls. I turned to the nurse and asked, "Do you have all your patients on computer?"

"Yes, we do, but these files have all the medical data on our patients," she said.

"We first need to find three patients in particular. Do you think you can extract their info from the computer to help us find where they are in this mess?" I asked.

She gave a smile to Deacon and said, "By the way, my name is Debbie, like in that movie 'Debbie Does Dallas.'" She winked at him and said to follow her. We went to a desk off to the side of the nurse's station and she sat, looked at me and said, "I need some names."

I gave her the three we had and she typed the info in then printed out a page containing the locations of their files. She stood and asked us to follow her back to the file room. She went to the file cabinets and pulled the files we needed then handed them slowly to Deacon. He said we didn't need her for now but to stay close. She said she would and left the room.

Deacon asked me if I could look over the files, too, for an extra perspective. Warren, Deacon and I sat at the table in the room as the two uniformed cops stood guard—from what, I didn't ask. We each took a file and opened them. I had Jessie's file. It was sad to read the information about her health exams and the notations about the bruises on her body since she was about six. Deacon had the Mexican woman's file, and it was sparse since she only came in once. Warren had the file on Noel, the youngest of the abuse victims. He asked, "What are we looking for?"

"Well, find out who was the attending doctor first," Deacon said and turned to me.

"I see the name of a Doctor Winston. He was the

doctor on call in Jessie's file," I replied.

"Same here, it's him in the child's file," Warren said.

"I've got him in Ramirez's file too. I think we have a common link." Deacon asked one of the cops to get Nurse Debbie again. He went out. She came breezing back in and right up to Deacon.

"You need me?" she asked.

"Yes, Debbie. Do you know where Doctor Steve Winston is at the moment?" he asked.

"Doctor Winston is no longer with us. He left about a month ago to go into private practice. Shall I get his address?"

"That would be great, I'd appreciate it."

She went out and we studied the files a bit more. I read the notations that Winston had placed in Jessie's file about the bruises. He was really disturbed by what he found. He also noted that he could not do much without the parents' consent but he knew they wouldn't give permission to have an investigation. I thought that doctors could report any findings of abuse to CPS. I'd have to check on that.

I turned to Deacon and said, "Look for times and dates of our patients being treated here and maybe we can cross reference with others who came in at the same time. We might get a fix on future victims."

Deacon agreed and Warren nodded. After checking our files, we all agreed that the files were similar as to the times and dates our abused victims were in for treatment. I wrote down the information.

The nurse came back in and handed Deacon a slip of paper with Winston's address. He read it and then turned a bit red. He looked at the girl and thanked her. We stood and went out of the room. I went after Deacon and asked why he was blushing.

"Nurse Debbie put her phone number on the paper and she wrote an almost obscene and possibly illegal suggestion. I didn't want to embarrass her or myself by making a big deal out of it, so I just wanted to get out of there."

"Can I see the paper?" I asked.

He walked away smiling and just said no.

**

Chapter 9

"Come on, just a peek," I begged. I almost collided into him when he stopped short of the nurse's station.

"I said no, let it go. Now can you think of anything else we might need while we still have the warrant?"

I stood thinking for a moment then asked Nurse Debbie who came up behind us, "Can you access the records as to dates when patients came in for exams?"

"Sure, our database can pull any info you need," she replied.

"Would you access the names and addresses of all patients who came in for treatment around this date?" I asked, handing her the paper on which I wrote the dates from our three files.

She looked at it and asked if I wanted a printout.

I said that would be good, so she went to the computer again and started to type.

"Just a quick peek," I asked Deacon again. He mouthed the word 'NO' silently. "I'll tell Lynn about the note," I joked.

"Go ahead, she's been hit on by many a perp, and she knows what effect a badge has on the opposite sex. Besides she knows I'd die if she found out I let any groupie carry out her wish."

Nurse Debbie came back with a stack of about a hundred sheets of paper full of names. I took them and thanked her. She winked at Deacon again and went off.

Deacon took the papers and handed them to Warren. "Have some of the guys do a search to see if any of the family members in this list are in our sex offender's database or reports of abuse." Warren took the list and went off.

"Let's get out of here before Nurse Debbie starts doing a strip tease."

"Just a peek," I asked.

"NO!"

~~*~~

Trapper was driving up Koval Avenue behind the casinos on the strip one road over. He was following Alicia Barnes as she pulled into the parking structure of the O'Shea's Casino next to the Flamingo Hotel and Casino. He wasn't sure if she was going to Flamingo or O'Shea's which was the smaller, more intimate of the two. She could also run across the street to Caesar's Palace or next door to Harrah's. He found a parking space on the third level just past where he saw Alicia park. They both got to the elevator at the same time. Trapper let her get on the car first and stood behind her as the thing went down to street level. Alicia gave him a smile as the doors opened and they went out.

"Excuse me, I hate to be forward, but could I ask you a favor?" she said to Trapper.

He gave his best smile and said sure.

She said, "I hate going in a casino alone. I get hit on by the lowlifes. Could you be so kind to escort me?"

He knew from yesterday when he followed her that she had no problem going into casinos alone. "I can sure do that, ma'am," he said.

"Please, call me Carol, and thank you. I feel safe with a big strong looking man like you."

He smiled and said, "What makes you think I wouldn't try hitting on you?" He probably would have too. She was very attractive, even under the extra make-up she wore. But he had to be professional. It was just a job, he told himself.

"Well, that's the chance I'll have to take," she said as she walked ahead up the alley from the parking structure to the strip. Trapper watched the nice rear end of the woman wiggling on her way and then followed her.

They were at the front entrance to O'Shea's and went in. O'Shea's was an older casino. It still had the flavor of the dark woods and was decorated like something out of early Vegas when the mob ruled the casinos. It was dark and a bit dingy but well maintained for one of the smaller casinos on the strip. Trapper followed Alicia, now calling herself Carol. He'd have to remember not to confuse the names. She headed straight to the roulette table after trading about a thousand dollars for chips at the cashier's booth.

She paused and said, "So, big guy, what's your name?"

Trapper smiled and said, "Jim." He loved the irony.

"Well, Jim, let's see if you are lucky."

She was betting small at first. The table limit was low, and she started to lose with each throw of the ball. She won a couple tosses and then started betting big. Trapper asked her what business was she in. She replied, "Hospitality. I work in different casinos to entertain guests."

"What sort of entertaining do you do, Carol?"

She gave him a sideways glance with a tilt of her head and said, "Anything a guest needs."

"Is this a free service?"

"Oh God no, I have to have my funds to run on. Nothing is free in Vegas anymore, not even the buffets."

"What could one expect to pay for your entertaining services?" he asked as she lost more money.

"Depends on what kind of entertainment you need. I can service you in many ways."

Trapper was experienced with hookers and escorts so he had to admit she was good. "That sort

60

of sounds like a proposition."

"Why, are you a cop?"

"Not anymore. I was in Detroit where I use to pull in entertaining ladies all the time. And I used to be a cop here in Vegas years ago."

She let out a coy little huff and said, "Oh, you wouldn't turn me in, now would you?"

"I hardly know you, so you're safe for now."

She smiled and lost the last of her chips. "Oh dear, I'm all out of chips. Would you like to contribute to my entertainment fund?"

"What's the price of good entertainment?"

"Anywhere from a hundred to a thousand. Do you want good entertainment or goood entertainment." She placed heavy emphasis on the last good.

"Well, I have business to do this afternoon, so I really have little time, but if you have a card or a location I could find you, I may consider goood entertainment."

She looked pouty and said, "Oh, I have to wait. Too bad, but I can fit you in later, if you know what I mean." She gave him a big smile and moved closer to brush her hand lightly on his crotch. Trapper stood his ground even though he wanted to take her right on the roulette table.

He looked at his watch and said, "Well, I'm running a little late for my business. Are you going to be all right alone with the lowlifes?"

"I think I'll survive. Here's my card. Call anytime you need entertainment." She kissed him on the cheek and then licked his ear. Trapper felt a chill and smiled.

"I'll definitely be in touch." He turned and left her at the table, but he went to the front of the small McDonald's next to the casino and waited to see if she was coming out. He waited for about ten minutes and then he saw her exiting with some guy with a crew cut wearing a Banlon pullover and khaki cargo pants. He reminded Trapper of the military personnel who came in from Nellis Air Base northeast of Vegas. He had his Minolta pocket camera out and snapped a few pictures of Alicia draping herself all over the guy. She wasn't very discreet so he could understand why she got hauled in for soliciting at the Golden Nugget. He followed them over to the Flamingo and up to the desk to get a room. He was being careful not to let Alicia spot him since she knew him. He'd have to resort to disguises now to follow her. They entered the elevator and he watched the lights go up to the fifth floor. Trapper had enough of her for the day and left the hotel.

He drove his car back to the office and went in to find Buck sitting at Lacey's desk. "You better not be fooling with her stuff. You know she doesn't like that." Trapper laughed.

"Nope, just playing receptionist for the day. I can do paperwork out here as well as in my office. Besides, the view out the windows is better here. I wish I had windows in my office."

Trapper smiled and went back to his office to print out the pictures.

~~*~~

Deacon and I drove over to Doc Winston's private practice on Charleston Boulevard just west of Rancho Drive. We parked in the lot on the side of the modest brick building sitting alone next to a bowling alley. We went in and found the waiting room was empty. The receptionist was sitting quietly reading a magazine and looked startled when we came in. "May I help you?" she asked.

Deacon pulled his badge and asked, "May we see Doctor Winston?"

She was quiet for a moment and said, "Aren't you here to tell me where he is?"

Deacon was taken aback by the statement and asked what she meant. She replied, "You're the police. Aren't you here to let me know where Doctor Winston is? He's been missing for the last week."

Deacon said, "I wasn't aware of him being missing. It's not my case. I wanted to ask him about a few patients he treated at the 6th Street clinic."

"Well, he's missing so you can't talk to him unless you can find him. As for his patients at 6th Street, he stopped working there last month, got fed up with all the pain and suffering from the indigents. Now he just takes cases of general practice or did until he vanished. He said all the abuse those poor people went through, he couldn't take it."

Deacon looked at me. "Maybe we found our vigilante."

**

Chapter 10

"Do you know the name of the primary investigator on the missing person case?" Deacon asked.

The woman sat thinking then said, "No."

"Okay, can you elaborate a bit? Where did he come from, North Vegas police?"

"Yes."

I said, "A woman of few words. Do you have a business card from the police in case the doc shows up here?"

"Oh, yes, I do," she said, opened her desk drawer, rummaged through the mess and finally found the card. "It's been almost a week since I got the card. They can go missing so easily." She handed it to Deacon.

He looked at the card and said, "Detective Maury Stoker, North Vegas police. Thank you, ma'am, this is a big help. Why are you still here if there is no business?"

"I have to answer the phone and tell patients that they have to wait till I call them."

"I see. Well, you have a nice day," Deacon said and turned to go out. I followed.

In the car Deacon said, "That woman is scary. Well, shall we go visit Maury?" We drove over to North Vegas precinct, which was over and up north on Las Vegas Boulevard, AKA 'the Strip,' and near Lake Mead Boulevard. It took us a short while to get there from our location.

We parked and went in the front entrance. Deacon was greeted by the desk officer. "Hey, Deacon, what brings you up to the good life?"

"Not your ugly mug. Are we still on for poker next Wednesday?" Deacon smiled as he went to the counter where the cop was standing.

"Yep, and bring plenty of cash, no more checks." He laughed.

"Tony, this is Jim Richards, P.I. and pain in the butt. Although he comes in handy once in a while," Deacon said.

"Oh, I know all about our famous investigator. He's pulled your butt out of the sling a few times." He shook my hand and continued, "I was in on the bride killer chase. Quite a stir that was."

I just smiled as Deacon asked, "Is Maury Stoker around?"

Tony looked at the callboard and said, "He's in, probably back in his cubicle. You know the place, down the hall and go right past Captain Sustaine's office. Just don't slow down around the captain's office. He's in a foul mood today."

"Thanks, Tony, see you Wednesday." Deacon led me into the squad room and quickly down the hall to missing persons. We found a cubicle with the nameplate saying Maury Stoker on it. Deacon turned into the cube and we found Stoker sitting at his computer looking at rap sheets. He was startled to see us.

"I presume you are Maury Stoker?" Deacon asked.

"In the flesh, and you are Deacon DeAngelo. I've

seen you around with your woman."

"Oh, don't call her my woman in front of her. She can hurt you bad." Deacon laughed.

"Noted. What can I do for you?"

"We need whatever you have on Doctor Steve Winston. Any progress on finding him?"

"Nothing definite. He's in the wind and I think he's hiding out. I found out from his girlfriend that he said he was threatened by some psycho about his wanting to tell the cops about the psycho's abuse of his wife. Psycho didn't like it and wanted to let the doc know that. We tracked down the psycho and he was all alibied up for any involvement in the doc's disappearance. He was in lock up down in your precinct for, what else, spousal abuse. He was in for about the first four days the doc disappeared. Psycho's name is Bert Frasher. He was just released two days ago and says he had no grudge against the doc. Yeah, right. I got men checking him out anyways. What's your interest?"

"I'm sure you've heard about the vigilante murders. He's a lead. We found the families of all three vics were all treated around the same time by the doc so we are looking seriously at him for the kills."

"Have you ever seen the doc?" Stoker asked.

"No, why?"

"I got his picture here," he said as he took out a photo from a file and handed it to Deacon. I looked over his shoulder. It showed a man with handicap crutches strapped to each arm. Stoker continued, "He's was shot up in Iraq as a medic. Those crazies

66

don't care if he had a red cross on. He was hit in the spine and can't walk without those crutches. So do you really think he could have murdered three men?"

Deacon was looking depressed as we now sat in his unmarked car. He held a copy of the doctor's picture and was just staring at it.

"Well, maybe he hired someone to commit the crimes," I said.

"That takes money to hire a hit man. I don't think the doctor has that kind of money, but I'll get Warren to run his financials. Well, where do we go now?" he said with a sigh. I knew he was hoping to solve the case to show Lynn he could do it on his own.

"We aren't beaten yet, just set back a step or two. We need to find out if Warren cross-referenced any of the lists you gave him to your database of sex offenders and reported abuses so we may have a lead on his next victim. It's getting late. Why don't we start fresh in the morning?" I said.

"Yeah, maybe we'll work better then. I'll drop you off at home and pick you up in the morning. Hopefully it will be a peaceful night." He pulled out of North Vegas precinct lot and across town to my home. He dropped me off and left. I saw that Penny's car was in the garage and went in. I was hoping they didn't bring home any horses. I went in and didn't find any horse pies in the living room and no smell. I went through to the back and found Penny and Jessie in the pool, naturally.

"Hey, Sweetie! How was your day relaxing?" Penny yelled to me from the side of the pool. Willy was swimming circles around Jessie who was laughing at the antics of the small dog.

"Hit a road block in our lead. Seems the guy we thought pulled the murders is handicapped, walks with crutches."

"Are you talking about Doctor Steve?" Jessie asked.

"Yes, he was your doctor wasn't he?" I asked back.

"He's a real nice doctor. He treated me well and talked to me about my dad and wanted to know what he was doing to me, but I didn't say because I knew my dad would beat me if I told." Holding onto a squirming Willy, she came over to the side next to Penny.

"So Doctor Steve was concerned for your safety?" I said.

"Yep, he told me he could get me into a nice place to help kids who are abused. I should have gone, but I knew that I would have ended back with my father if things didn't work out. I didn't need more trouble, so I said no."

"Did Doctor Steve ever say anything to you about his life, where he lived or his interests?" I asked.

"He said he liked the water around Lake Mead. He had a cabin there he would go to when he wanted to get away," she replied.

Well, it was something. "Thanks, Jessie. Did you have a good time at Penny's station with the knights?"

"Oh yes, I even got to sit on one of the jousting horses. They were huge," she said with a really toothy grin.

Penny laughed and said, "Jessie and Lacey both got to meet with the king and queen of the Excalibur Hotel show. We had a good time, didn't we Jessie?"

"Yep," she said as Willy squirmed out of her arms and took off in the water, followed by Jessie. Penny climbed out and came to me as I sat on one of the plastic chairs.

She kissed me and plopped down on my lap making me wet in the process. "Thanks, I needed cooling off." I tilted my head back and looked at the big temperature gauge on the side of the house. It was ninety-five degrees. I looked back at Penny. "I'll be glad when it's officially summer. Then the temperature will get into the hundreds."

"You are a crazy person." She wiggled her butt and then stood, picked up her towel and started to dry off.

We ate a quick meal nuked in the microwave, had our chips and refreshments and watched TV. Around ten I said I had to get up early to go investigate with Deacon.

Penny said, "It's Saturday. You're going to work on my day off?"

"I think Deacon needs a little extra help with this case. I think he's trying to prove to Lynn he can do the job without her."

"Well, then go help him. I usually feel sorry for him following Lynn around as she takes lead on all the cases. Even if she is the lieutenant, he needs to get some glory too."

"You are correct, so I give up my day off and

help my friend," I said.

"You are such a humanitarian. You should get a plaque," she said with a smirk.

"I keep saying that," I replied.

~~*~~

Bert Frasher was pissed that he spent the better part of the week in jail all because the nosy neighbors had called the police about his altercation with his wife. "Damn bitch deserved to get her ass beat," he mumbled to himself. "None of anybody else's business, damn people." Bert was standing outside his apartment building peeing in the bushes. He finished and zipped, then reached down to get the long neck beer he had set on the sidewalk. An elderly couple was walking up the sidewalk to their apartment and cast their eyes to him as they came by. "What the hell you looking at, you old fuckers?" he yelled. They moved a bit quicker and were around the corner before he turned to see a dark man standing in the shadows between the buildings. The figure waved to him and then gave him the finger. That pissed off Bert and he yelled, "Hey, you can't do that to me!"

The man turned and went off into the darkness. Bert headed towards the man in a shaky sprint from the beer he had consumed most the day. He came around a corner and was whacked in the head by an arm. He went down, hard. The dark figure grabbed his arms, pulled them behind his body, and secured them with a plastic wire wrap. The figure then unbuckled Bert's belt and pulled down his pants, turned the man on his stomach and inserted the long neck bottle in Bert's ass. He pumped it hard and fast a few times as Bert screamed.

The man gave Bert's head a wicked twist and Bert went silent. He was dead.

**

Chapter 11

"Okay, this doesn't make sense. Frasher was murdered early this morning after being released from lock up two days ago and now he's dead. He threatened Doc Winston, but Winston is not capable of doing this," Deacon said, looking down at the body of Frasher still butt naked. "That must have hurt. Ouch!"

I was smiling as I watched Deacon stalking around the area looking for anything. Forensics had already released the crime scene and ME Joe Lang was still doing his thing.

The area was taped off and there were a good number of uniformed cops keeping the resident lookie-loos back. The news vultures were all straining to get their shots and sound bytes, but Frasher was behind a porch fence of an apartment so they couldn't get his image very well. Besides, in his position they'd have to blur his ass in the picture for TV.

The EMTs came with a gurney and the famous black bag. They bundled him up and put him on the gurney then took him away. "Joe, aren't you going to pull the bottle out?" I asked.

"Hell no. This wife beater can go to the morgue the way we found him. Good for the vigilante. The lab can have the bottle after I get him to the morgue." He didn't smile, he just went off.

"I'm seeing a pattern here. This murderer is becoming a hero," I said to myself.

Deacon came up to me. "We should go see what Warren came up with from the list. We don't have much else to go on."

"Well, I may have a small lead. Jessie told me last night that the doc said he had a cabin at Lake Mead."

"Really? I'll call Maury Stoker and see if he has that info." He pulled his cellphone and pushed a button. He asked for Stoker and waited. "Maury, this is Deacon. I got some info on Winston. Do you know about a cabin he has at Lake Mead?" He paused for a few moments, listening. "Well, let me know what you find. I still need to talk to the doc about the threat. Your psycho Frasher came up dead this morning. I really need to talk to the doc now."

~~*~~

Trapper was sitting in his office when he received the call. He answered and heard a very distraught voice. "Mr. Trapper, it's Chester Barnes. Do you know where my wife is?"

"Didn't she come home last night? I left her at the Flamingo Hotel which I was going to call you about."

"No, she didn't come home and I don't know what to do. Should I call the police?"

"They won't do anything until she's been gone for at least forty-eight hours. Let me do some checking around for you. Are you at home?"

"Yes, I called in sick this morning until I know she's safe. Please help. I'm out of my mind worrying about her."

"Okay, just relax and call me if you hear from her. I'll see what I can do to find her and be in touch." They finished and hung up. He decided to wait on telling Barnes about his wife's hooking until he knew more of what was going on. Trapper dialed his friend Josh Harper and asked if he could help track down the woman he asked about yesterday.

"You lost her?" Josh asked.

"I watched her go into the Flamingo Hotel elevator with some john. Yes, she's hooking for the money, and it was the last I saw of her."

"Flamingo? Was this in the afternoon?"

"Yeah it was about three when I left. Why?"

"Let me get back to you. I heard there was a murder in one of the suites. A woman was brought in. I'll see who she is and call you back." He hung up and Trapper sat back, hoping it wasn't his client's wife.

~~*~~

Vegas Vigilante Murders

Deacon drove up to his precinct as I followed in my car since he had called me at home to say he was at the crime scene and I drove there. It was a Saturday morning. Penny and Jessie were still trying to sleep, so I went out quietly. I did write a note for Penny and left it on the snack bar. We arrived at Metro precinct and went in.

"Warren, you got anything on the list I gave you yesterday?" he asked the detective as we came up to his desk in the squad room.

"We narrowed the names down to about five who had records or reports of abuse or sexual activities. Two of them are in prison and we're tracking down the others." He handed the list to Deacon who smiled and said they could take Bert Frasher's name off the list.

"You know where he is?" Warren asked.

"Yep, on ice in the morgue. He was murdered this morning."

"This guy is maintaining a schedule. Four kills in four days. We had better find the other two men on the list. If he hits those men, does he stop there or does he have another list that he's working from?" Warren asked.

"Good question. This is just from our investigation of the doc at 6th Street. He was our prime suspect, but he's handicapped and missing, so where does that leave us?" Deacon said.

"Get anything from the lab?"

"Not yet. I'm going to call them after I visit Joe Lang in his chamber of horrors." Deacon smiled and took me to the morgue.

Bob Moats

I had been in the morgue once before. I never cared much for the smells, and the temperature was low so I wasn't comfortable with that either. We came through a door after putting on the gown and masks that were made mandatory after a few cases were contaminated by visitors to the morgue. Joe was happily cutting up the naked body of Frasher and putting his internals in the various trays he had on the stainless steel counters that surrounded the slab holding the body. I stopped back a ways from the table. I wasn't that interested in seeing a man cut up. Lang looked up and said, "Wondered when you'd be in, Deacon."

"I had to take care of a few details. What have you got?"

"Well, he had a long, narrow bruise on the side of his face. Probably knocked down with an arm or bat. His wrists were tied, his pants pulled down and the bottle was forced into his cavity and given a few good thrusts. Then the perp gave a twist to his head which snapped it, and he was dead. The perp is either strong or knows what he's doing. Is that simple enough?"

"Glad you didn't go into all those big fancy terms you medical people use on us dumb cops." Deacon smiled under the mask.

"I never use fancy terms, you know that. I hate wasting time talking like some fancy TV or murder book coroner. Ah jus' be a simple boy."

"Did you find anything on the body that could give us a lead?"

"Nope, this perp was careful to cover his tracks.

I'd say he wore rubber gloves to do his deed. I did find powder on him from that looked like the stuff they put on rubber gloves, but I won't know until trace examines it. Nothing much more to tell you, so excuse me. I have work to do since I have a backup of bodies here."

We went out, tossed our scrubs in the trash, and went back up to Lynn's office. "Have you heard from Lynn lately?" I asked.

"Every night. She's miserable being away but starting to enjoy the course she's taking. It's covering all forms of law enforcement and she said she's learning some good stuff."

"You think she'll survive being away for the month?"

"Yeah, she's tough. She'll make it, but I don't know if I can hold out."

"Lack of sex getting to you?"

He just smiled and picked up the desk phone, saying he was calling the lab. He dialed a number and asked for someone named Barb Benton, waited and then said who he was. "Barb, have you got anything from the four vigilante murders for me?" He listened and then hung up.

"Damn, forensics has nothing. Not one thing that can give us a heads up on this guy," he said quietly. His cell phone rang and he answered. "Hey, Maury, got something for me? I'm spinning my wheels here." He listened for a moment and then hung up, smiling.

"Maury said the Lake Mead sheriffs out of Boulder Beach went to the doc's cabin near Saddle Island and found him. He's alive and well. But he can't be our murderer. They say he had an alibi for this last week. Seems there was a woman he was shacking up with despite the fact he has a girlfriend here in Vegas. Turns out he just wanted to get away from it all and didn't feel threatened by anyone. So he says."

"He just disappears off to his cabin without saying a word to anyone? Seems fishy to me," I said.

"Maury says he's driving out there to have a talk with him. He'll let me know what he finds."

Trapper was on the phone with Sam, AKA Samantha, the former call girl and now bookie, whom he had met while he was helping to catch the Black Widow killer. Trapper had been seeing her for the last month, not anything serious but Trapper had a thing for ladies of the night, even former ones. He was setting up a time for them to get together for dinner one night when his cell phone rang. He begged off on his call to Sam and hung up. He answered. It was Josh.

"Trapper, got some news on your missing, gambling wife. She's in lock up for murder."

**

Chapter 12

Deacon and I looked over the cut down list of predators that Warren had narrowed, and we decided to go chase the only two names left on the list. Deacon pulled a nice Dodge Charger police interceptor out of the police motor pool and we drove to the closest address of the two men on the list.

We arrived at a rundown house on Vista Drive and parked out front. The house had the desert landscaping that the county asked people to use instead of the water hungry lawns many people still had. The Vegas area was in a drought situation and people were being paid to put out rocks and desert plants in front of their houses instead of grass and shrubs.

We walked up to the house as the front door flew open and a small boy about twelve or so came bursting out. Behind him, screaming at the top of his lungs, was a man calling the boy a good number of nasty names. The man stopped when he saw us near the porch.

"What the hell do you want? We don't need no religion here, so go thump your bibles elsewhere. I got a kid to beat!" He started after the boy when Deacon tackled him and swung him around to the ground. "What the hell are you doing?" the man protested.

"Sir, you are under arrest for threatening and attempted assault on a minor child. Hold still or I'll break your arm!" Deacon yelled in the man's ear.

"Oh, man, don't pull this on me. I just got out of the slammer. I don't need to go back," he wailed.

"Well, you should have thought of that before you decided to go after the kid," Deacon said.

I looked over to where the boy had run to and saw him standing behind a car watching Deacon cuff the man. I walked to the boy and called to him, "Hi, you can come back. He won't hurt you now."

He didn't seem to want to move so I went to him. "Hi, my name is Jim, and you are?"

The boy stood quietly then said, "I'm Tommy."

"Well, Tommy, is that your father?" I asked as Deacon threw the man in the enclosed back of the police car.

"No, my stepfather. I hate him."

"It's OK now. My friend is a cop and he is going to take your stepfather in. Can you tell us what was happening?" I said as Deacon came up to us.

"I was trying to make a sandwich and spilled the jelly. He got mad and said I was wasting his food. He came after me and I ran. He's always beating on me. Can you lock him up for good?" he said as he looked at Deacon.

"Well, we can't keep him forever unless he did something really bad," Deacon said with a smile.

"How about if he's growing weed?" the boy said quickly.

"Well, that might do it. May we look in the house?"

The boy nodded and took us to the front door. Deacon stopped and asked, "Do you live here, Tommy?"

"Yes, with that bastard in your car. My mom moved out."

"Okay, Tommy, then you are allowing us to enter your house to see this garden of weed?"

"Yeah, you can come in."

I knew it would be better if Deacon was invited into the house. He didn't need a search warrant that way. We went in and the boy took us to the back of the house and to the enclosed porch where we found about a dozen or more marijuana plants growing tall and strong.

"Does your mom help with this?" Deacon asked.

"No, like I said, she doesn't live here now. She moved out to live with her biker friends, and they come here for the weed. I had to stay here because the bikers didn't want me there. I just stayed in my room and out of his way," he said looking in the direction of Deacon's car.

Deacon pulled his cell phone, called for backup and CSI to check the house. Deacon said we should go wait out front until they arrived. We were standing on the front porch talking when two patrol cars and a CSI SUV pulled up. Deacon went out and explained what we found and how we found it. The one uniform I knew as Tim and his partner came in and started to do a search. CSI went out back to the porch as Deacon told them where to go. Tim's partner taped off the house at the porch.

We went out with Tommy and stood waiting as the officers did their job. Tim came out and said, "Looks like this guy was busy. We found weapons and cash stashed in a room at the back and a number of bags of a substance that looked like cocaine. CSI is bagging it all."

Deacon let Tim and his partner put the man in their patrol car, and Deacon turned to me. "Well, it's one less person the vigilante will get to."

We waited for Tommy's mom to show up after we got her number from Tommy. I felt sorry for the boy after seeing her show up. She looked strung out and she was complaining that she didn't have a place to take him to. Deacon suggested CPS and she gave him a look like he had sworn at her.

"I'm not giving my son to those bastards. I'll keep him here with me as long as that idiot I married doesn't come back. Besides, I need to get away from the scum I'm living with. We're not getting along." She turned to the house and was told by Tim that she couldn't stay there until the house was cleared and released. She wailed about not having any place to take the boy.

"Excuse me," I said to her. "Take him and yourself to a motel for now. The police will let you know when you can move back in." I took out enough cash to put them in a motel for a few days, gave the money to Tim, and asked him if he could take them to a motel and get them a room. I didn't trust her to take the money. He said he would and told her to follow him in her car.

They drove off and Deacon said, "You didn't have to do that."

"I know, but Penny would kill me if I brought home a new kid." I laughed.

Vegas Vigilante Murders

~~*~~

Trapper arrived at Metro precinct just as Chester Barnes pulled up. "I can't believe that my wife is involved in murder. That is not like her," he said after he parked and came up to Trapper who had called him to meet at the precinct.

"Chester, I need to tell you a few things about your wife. I'm sorry to be the one to say this but your wife was prostituting herself for the cash to gamble."

"You have to be wrong, Mr. Trapper. My wife would not do that."

"Well, she propositioned me in O'Shea's." Trapper took out the pocket recorder he had running while he was talking to Alicia Barnes in O'Shea's. He played the recording for him as he stood looking pale.

"I can't believe she would go to this extreme for her gambling."

"Mr. Barnes, it's an addiction and people with a gambling addiction will do anything to get a fix, just like a drug addict. She needs help and understanding. We have to find out about the murder charges and see what you need to do to get her bailed out." Trapper led Barnes into the precinct and met with his friend, Detective Josh Harper, at his desk.

"Hey, Josh, this is Chester Barnes, Alicia's husband. What's the word?"

Harper asked Barnes to sit in the chair next to his desk and pulled a file. "Well, Chester, may I call you Chester?" He got a nod and continued, "Your wife was found screaming in the hallway of the Flamingo

Hotel and when security arrived, they found a man dead in the bed of her room. She said she went in to take a long shower and by the time she came out, she found the guy still in bed, dead. She figured he was dead by the blood all around him on the bed and walls, but she says she never touched him. She then came out into the hallway calling for help, which is where security found her, sitting on the floor in the middle of the hall, crying. First cops on the scene took over from the hotel security and determined that she is the main suspect and they figured she murdered the guy then she washed up. Don't have the reports back yet from forensics, so they brought her in to cool overnight. Hotel security ran the camera footage back and no one entered the room after they went in up to the time Alicia came out of the room. I'm not primary on the case but I can keep tabs on it for you. Detective Mike Dabney is primary and he'll want to talk to you. I'll let him know you are here."

Trapper asked, "Who was the man in the bed?"

"He was a flight specialist from Nellis, Art Kramer. He was the Air Force's man in charge of all flights in and out of the air base to points around the world. He also was in charge of cargo manifests and routing. I got a couple of my guys out there talking to his superiors and co-workers. The Air Force is conducting their own investigation, but we have jurisdiction since it happened in the city."

Josh Harper looked up to Trapper, then to Barnes. "You can go talk to your wife now if you'd like."

**

Chapter 13

Deacon and I went back to the car and drove out to the next address for the other name on the possible victim's list. We went across town to Charleston and Rainbow Boulevard then into a subdivision of nice homes, all in a higher income bracket. I was intrigued that someone with any amount of money would be an abuser of spouse or child, but I realized that there were even murderers with good incomes out there. We pulled up to a colonial style house complete with columns of white framing the veranda that crossed the front of the house.

We walked up to the house and the door opened just as we stepped on the porch. A woman in her late forties came out looking concerned. "Are you men with the police?" she asked.

Deacon had a puzzled look and said, "Yes, ma'am, I am. I'm Detective DeAngelo and this is Jim Richards, civilian advisor. Were you expecting the police?"

"Yes, I was. I got a call that my husband was killed yesterday and a police detective was coming to talk to me. Are you him?"

"No, ma'am, we came to see if we could get some information about abuse charges and if you went to the 6th Street clinic?"

She stood looking dazed like she would faint. Deacon went to her. "Ma'am, you look like you should sit down."

"Yes, I'm not well, thank you." She turned and

went back in as we followed. She went to the living room just off the vestibule and sat on an easy chair, then she pulled a handkerchief from a pocket and dabbed her eyes as they started watering. "I'm sorry. I have been going through hell this morning waiting for the detective to show. My husband didn't come home last night, and then I was called and told that Arthur was found dead in the Flamingo Hotel. The person who called said he was a detective and would be out to talk to me. You know nothing about this?"

"I'm sorry, but we didn't know about your husband. We came here in regards to another case I'm working on. Have you heard on the news about the vigilante murders?"

She looked shaken and then just stared. "Yes, I heard about them. I thought this was about my husband. He fit in with what the news said about the killings. He was a violent man. He beat our son and me all too often. Our son left home when he turned of consenting age. That left me to be the punching bag. When I got the call, I thought the vigilante had gotten Arthur."

"I'm sorry for your loss. I guess that answers what I wanted to ask. But I need to know if you were treated by a Doctor Winston in the last year."

She turned her head to Deacon and said, "He was my doctor at the clinic on Charleston. He had just moved there from the mission clinic. He is a very nice man. I liked his concern for my wellbeing in regards to the abuse I took from Arthur."

Deacon looked at me and nodded. There was a knock at the door and Mrs. Kramer jumped. Deacon said he would get the door. She thanked him. He went and looked out the door window to the porch and saw a man waiting. He opened the door and the man looked surprised.

"Hey, you're DeAngelo, aren't you?"

"Yep, and you're Carl Garity."

"That I am. What are you doing here? Are you on the case too?"

"If you're referring to Kramer's murder, I'm not here for that. I'm on the vigilante killings. Come on in."

"Well, so you think this case ties into your case? Is the wife here?"

"Yeah, come on into the living room." Deacon led the detective to where I sat with Mrs. Kramer. Deacon introduced Garity to me then said, "Ma'am, this is Detective Garity. He's the person you were expecting."

She looked at Garity and asked, "Do you have anything about my husband you can tell me?"

Garity sat in the chair Deacon had vacated so Deacon sat on a couch by the woman. Garity sat for a moment, probably organizing his thoughts, and then said, "We received a report that a man was found dead in a room at the Flamingo Hotel. He was with a woman who we determined to be a prostitute and at first theorized that she killed him. But forensics cannot find any connection to his death. She was cleared of the murder. We were trying to piece together what may be a cause for his murder, which is why I need to ask you a few questions."

Deacon said, "Carl, I think this fits in with my

86

case of the vigilante killings. Mrs. Kramer was telling me she thought he murdered her husband because he fit the profile. He was an abuser and that's who our vigilante is going after. Did the hooker say if she saw who did this?"

"No, she says she was in the shower when he was killed and came out after. She drew the attention of hotel security. She could have just run but didn't. There are more things we need to find out about the woman before we can release her." He looked back to the woman. "Mrs. Kramer, can you come into the precinct to identify your husband? I can drive you."

"Yes, I can go. I'll need to close up here and then we can leave." She stood and went to the hall and off to get ready.

"So you think this is the vigilante's work?"

Deacon said, "It fits. We came here because Kramer was on our list of possible vics for the vigilante. Now he turns up dead. You make the connection."

Trapper and Barnes sat in Detective Mike Dabney's office as the detective was talking. "Mr. Barnes, we have pretty much cleared your wife for the murder. CSI did a thorough check of her and could find no trace of blood splatter on her. The way the man was murdered, she would have been covered in it. Even with the shower, she would have had something if she had perpetrated the crime. Were you aware that your wife was having sex with other men?"

"No, I wasn't. She has a gambling addiction as Mr. Trapper has explained. I hired Mr. Trapper from the Richards Investigation firm to follow my wife and see if she was gambling. He found she was and that she had tried to stir up some funds by having sex for money. He says she may have done this for the cash to gamble."

"Well, Mr. Barnes, it's not unusual for people to steal or prostitute themselves for quick cash to gamble. The problem now is between your wife and yourself. There are a good number of counselors around Vegas that can help. Since there was nothing mentioned by the arresting officers about cash for sex, there will be no charges. She's had a rough enough time as it is."

"When can I get my wife?"

"We just have a few more preliminary things to do then we will be releasing her to you. Figure about an hour."

"Thank you," Barnes said.

Trapper asked, "Does this murder have anything to do with the vigilante killings?"

"Not that I know of but we still have to do some interviews and checking. Anything is possible." Dabney stood and said, "I won't need you anymore, so you can go to the holding area and your wife will be released there."

Trapper and Barnes stood, shook Dabney's hand and went out. Trapper was familiar with the precinct from having worked there years before so he led Barnes to where he would pick up his wife. They sat in the lobby waiting until a door opened and a big cop led Alicia out. She saw her husband and just stood looking ashamed. She saw Trapper and her eyes got big. She came to them.

"What are you doing here?" she demanded of Will.

Barnes stepped up and said, "He's working for me, a private investigator. That's not the issue. What the hell were doing having sex and gambling?"

She looked away and started to tear up. Barnes pulled her to a chair and sat her down. He sat next to her. "I'm going to help you through this but you have to want to cooperate. For God's sake, you were involved in a murder. You could have been killed or seriously injured. This is going to stop now. Things will have to change."

She looked up at him, her eyes red, and said, "I need help, Chester. I can't stop. You have to help me."

"I will, I will help."

Trapper said, "I'll leave you two to sort out your lives. I'm done." Barnes thanked him and Trapper walked away.

~~*~~

Deacon and I were entering the back door of Metro precinct just as Trapper was coming out. He looked a little surprised. Deacon said, "What are you doing here, Will?"

"I was just bringing in Chester Barnes to see his wife. She was arrested yesterday while involved in a murder at the Flamingo Hotel."

Deacon and I just looked at each other and smiled. "Was the murdered victim named Arthur Kramer?" I asked.

He said yes with a puzzled expression. "What do you know of the murder?" he asked.

"Your gambling wife was involved with a victim of our vigilante," I answered.

Will said, "Well, this just keeps getting better, doesn't it?"

**

Chapter 14

The three of us went back into Lynn's office. "Okay, no one saw the murder of Art Kramer, so we don't positively know it was the vigilante. Alicia Barnes was in the shower when it happened and the hotel security cameras didn't get anyone coming or going to the room. Now if it was the doc, how could a handicapped man slip in and out to commit murder?" Deacon threw the question out to Trapper and me.

"Are there pass through doors between the rooms?" I asked.

Trapper said, "Most of the hotels do have them. The Flamingo does."

"So that's our first option. Can you get security camera video of the adjoining rooms?" I asked

Deacon. He said it was worth a try and yelled out to Warren.

"Yeah, Deacon," he said as he popped up at the door. Then he saw Trapper. "Hey, Will, what's shaking?"

"Not much, Greg, thanks."

"Can you go check out the video at the Flamingo for people entering rooms on either side of the room where Kramer was killed? Be sure to talk to Mike Dabney. It's his case. Just to stay on the good side of everyone."

"Sure, can do," he said and went off.

Deacon leaned back in Lynn's chair and sighed. I said, "Don't get too comfortable there. Lynn will know you fooled with her chair."

"Yeah, but she'll get over it."

"Have you two talked much more about marriage?" I asked.

"Yep, she's all for it, but if we do, they may separate us. I don't know if I can get away with as much goofing off as I do now in another area. I'd have to really work," he said with a laugh.

Trapper said, "Don't go messing up a good thing with marriage. Divorces can get messy."

Deacon's cell phone rang and he nearly fell back in the chair. He steadied himself and answered. "Hello," he said, then listened. "Thanks, I'll go take a look." He hung up then stood and went to the door. "That was Dabney. He said they got a call to the local TV stations that the vigilante killer is making a statement." He left the room. Trapper and I got up and followed wherever he was heading. We found

Vegas Vigilante Murders

Deacon in the break room standing in front of the TV there. He had a breaking news bulletin showing on the screen.

"...the phone call came in a half hour ago and our calls to the LVMPD were not responded to. They defer to investigating the call and will make a statement later. The caller identified himself as the Vegas Vigilante and said he was going to take his vengeance out for those victims of abuse who can't stand up for themselves. He listed the men he has murdered in the last five days, all accounted for including the death of Arthur Kramer yesterday in the Flamingo Hotel. This is the call that was made. Listen closely in case you may recognize the voice." She looked off to the side and the screen showed the words across the bottom saying it was the voice of the vigilante.

"People of Las Vegas, I am the Vegas Vigilante and I want to make a statement as to my purpose of bringing justice to the women and children who have been victimized by abuse from a family member or someone they know. I have put five men to their death for their crimes. I will continue finding more of these criminals and completing my quest to rid the world of these scum. Don't think you can get away with brutalizing human beings. The police can't do much if the victims will not stand up against these cruel heartless people. So I will stand up for them. Beware."

The screen went back to the anchor and she said, "The police have been silent on this and have no comments so far. We will be watching and will keep you informed." The screen changed and there was a commercial for a show at the MGM Grand. Deacon reached up and turned off the TV, looked at us and said, "This could get bad. I'm thinking that abused wives may now kill their husbands and claim it was the vigilante. We need to find this guy."

"Maybe that's his intention. He kills off a few bad guys then lets the tide roll on," Trapper said.

"Well, we'll find out if we have another kill tomorrow, and since Kramer, we're out of leads," Deacon replied.

"Can we at least go visit the doc and see what he has to say?" I asked.

"It can't hurt. I'll call Maury Stoker and get the doc's location," Deacon said as he picked up the desk phone. After he talked to Maury, Deacon told Warren where he was going and a few minutes later the three of us were heading to the motor pool for a car.

The drive to Lake Mead took us the better part of an hour the way Deacon drove. He pulled the charger interceptor again and made good time on the journey. We pulled up to the sheriff's station and got out, a courtesy call to let them know we were in town to investigate. We entered the small building that had three cars out front. I assumed they didn't have many officers. Deacon flashed his badge and asked for Herman Heron, the deputy in charge of the station. We were led to his office.

"Gentlemen, have a seat. How can I help Vegas' finest investigators, or was that the detectives who came through yesterday?" Heron laughed.

Deacon smiled and said, "We want to talk to

Vegas Vigilante Murders

Doctor Winston as part of our investigation of the vigilante murders. We just wanted to give you a heads up as to our presence here. Just a courtesy to your fine work." Then Deacon grinned.

Heron laughed loud and then said, "Okay, you have made your presence known. Now what can I tell you about the doc?"

"How long have you known him?" Deacon asked.

"He's been a model citizen for about four years and even processed a few bodies for us that popped up here. Yes, we do have crime out here in paradise. He's been holed up for the last week or so with his girlfriend, Heather. She's a dancer from Vegas, works in one of the casino shows, the topless kind. But she's a decent girl, everyone likes her."

Deacon thought about his sister, Maria. She danced topless even though Deacon wasn't fond of it. "So the doc has been here all week and no one ever saw him head out of town?"

"Not that we know, but we don't watch the doc closely. Go talk to him, see what you think. Just keep me informed."

"Thanks, we'll keep you in the loop. We need to stop the vigilante before all hell breaks loose in Vegas," Deacon said.

"Yep, now it's open season on abusers, isn't it?" the deputy said.

"You got that right," Deacon said and we offered our good-byes and left the building. Back on the road, out of town and around the lake to the address we had for Doctor Winston. It was more of a chalet-type cabin than a home. We pulled into the long drive that took us to the side of the building facing the lake. It was beautiful, calm, and the temperature was just right, not like the one hundred plus degrees in Vegas.

Deacon was first out of the car. Trapper and I took our time getting out. We were letting Deacon take lead on our little quest. He arrived at the door and knocked since there was no doorbell. We came up as the door opened. There stood a gorgeous woman in dancer's tights. She smiled.

"May I help you?" she asked. I could tell Trapper was drooling at the sight of her.

Deacon turned his head back to Trapper with a look like he should behave. He turned back to Heather and said, "Hi, I'm Detective Frank DeAngelo, LVMPD. These men are private investigators and civilian advisors to the Las Vegas police. We're here to see Doctor Winston. Is he in?"

"No, he's on a call for a sick woman in town. Is this about his disappearance that the police talked to him about yesterday?"

"Well, ma'am, we're here to talk to him about his work at the 6th Street clinic. Do you know when he'll be back?"

"Come on in. He called and said he was on his way back."

Deacon told her the cabin was very nice, and she said to call her Heather. She asked, "Can I offer you some tea or coffee?

We politely told her no and she asked us to sit in the small living room. She said she had to change and went off into the house as we sat looking around the room. It was very cozy, all wood decor, huge fireplace and many cushions on the chairs and couch. I smiled to myself thinking how Penny would like this.

Heather came back in the room quickly, probably from being able to change quickly for her shows. I asked, "Heather, where do you dance at?"

"I'm a dancer for the Tropicana. It's a great place to work," she bubbled.

Deacon perked up and said, "Do you know Maria DeAngelo?"

"I wondered when you said your name if you knew Maria. Yes, we are friends. Are you her brother?" she asked.

"Yes, I am."

"Well, I can see what she was talking about, you being a great looking guy. Too bad you are living with the lady cop," she said with a smile.

"Yes, I'm living with a lady cop. Now can I ask you a few questions?" he said, changing the subject.

"Sure, anything for Maria's brother."

"Thanks. Can you tell me all you know about Steve Winston?"

**

Chapter 15

"I really hate to talk about him when he's not here," she replied.

"I understand, but I just need to know if he's been here with you all week."

"Yes, other than the few times he went to comfort someone who's sick. He gets lots of calls for that even though he's trying to relax out here."

"How long is he gone when he goes to help people?" I asked.

"Usually about an hour, less sometimes. Depends on what's wrong with the person he's seeing."

I looked at Deacon and said, "Not enough time to get to Vegas and back, even if he drove faster than you." I smiled when I said it.

Deacon had a strange look on his face, as if he was constipated. "Yes, he would have to go really fast. Tell me, Heather, does he talk much about the patients he had at the 6th Street clinic?"

"I can answer that for you, Detective." A voice came from the hallway as the doctor came quietly in on his crutches. "Hello, gentlemen, I'm Doc Winston. Now you can talk to me. If this is about my being missing, I'm not. I'm here, so what is it you want?"

Deacon stood as the doctor made his way to the couch and sat. "Please sit and be comfortable," the doc said.

Deacon sat and said, "We are investigating the murders of five men in the last five days by a person who calls himself the Vegas Vigilante."

"And what does that have to do with me?"

"Well, all the persons murdered were part of families treated by you at the 6th Street clinic. We have to follow up on connections, and since you are one of those connections we have to ask you about these people." Deacon took out his note pad and read off the names of the people who were treated by the doc. He sat nodding as each name was called.

"Yes, I know these people. I have treated them and they were all abused in one way or another by those men you mentioned. But as you see I couldn't possibly be the vigilante. I can barely get around on these things," he said, looking at his crutches.

"We've already ruled you out as a suspect, but you may be able to help by telling us anything you may know that could aid us in finding this killer."

"Yes, he's a killer, but I'd say he's more of an executioner, like they have in prisons. I am a doctor and life is sacred to me, but I find comfort in knowing these men will never raise a hand to another person. You understand what I mean. No, I would never take a life no matter how evil the person is, so I can't really tell you much. I have no information that could help you to find this person. Since I can't help you, I have nothing more to say. I'm tired from running around today so if you could excuse us, please."

Deacon took his cue and thanked the doctor and Heather then stood, followed by Trapper and me as we departed their home.

It was starting to get late and we were all worn

from the long day. We were quiet on the trip back. Deacon pulled into the police motor pool and we left the car and stood in the parking lot. Deacon spoke first. "So where do we go now?"

"Who's examining the phone call that came in today?" Trapper asked.

"I'm sure it's in the lab by now. I don't know who pulled it, and they should have called me since it's my case. I'll find out and let you guys know later. I think we need to take a break and go home."

We said our good-byes. Trapper just said he would see us later. He still refused to say good-bye. At least I knew why since he told me that he lost two loved ones after he harshly said good-bye so he never said it again to persons he cared about.

I went to my car after telling Trapper that I'd see him in the morning at the office and drove home to Penny and Jessie. I pulled into the drive and went in to hear the drive alarm going off. I went to reset the thing and wondered where the girls were. I heard Willy yip in the back and went out, passing the ugly statue but pausing long enough to feed the goldfish. Penny was helping Jessie to swim, and Willy was sitting on the side watching them. Willy looked at me and ran up letting me lift him. I went to the plastic chairs.

Penny saw me. "Hi, Sweetie. How was your day?"

"Very long and full of bad people. I'll tell you about it later." I relaxed and was petting Willy as he lay on my lap.

Jessie gave me a big smile and said, "I'm getting

better at swimming now. I really like this. Watch!" She swam off down the long length of the pool and back. I applauded her as she came back to the side by Penny.

They got out of the pool and dried off. I asked if they had eaten anything and Penny said they went to In-N-Out for burgers. I realized I hadn't eaten all day. I was busy and didn't have time to eat, so I went into the house to raid the fridge. I ended up with two tuna on toasted Kaiser rolls and some potato salad that tasted like it was on its last legs. I sat at the snack bar eating the rolls and tossing the salad. Penny and Jessie had gone off to change and we ended up on the couch watching a couple comedies on TV. Jessie was tired so she excused herself to go to bed. I told Penny about my day.

"So you have no leads for who this vigilante is?"

"Nope, and Deacon is hoping that our list was the last of the victims to be murdered. If there are more, we'll have to rethink our list."

"You said you were going by the listings from the 6th Street clinic, but maybe the killer has a list from other clinics also. Maybe he's someone who has an inside track on the clinics but doesn't actually work there. Am I making sense?"

"Actually you are. It could be an administrator of medical treatments that have to be reported by the clinics to keep track of what's going on. I'm just talking out my ass here since I have no idea what kind of position would have connections to more clinics."

"Maybe a salesman from a drug company. They

go into clinics every day to push their drugs. Maybe they snoop the patient's lists for people to rub out."

"Rub out? What are you, a mob moll now?"

"I watch the good crime shows so I know the vernacular."

"Rub out, that's something you'd hear in the old black and white flicks."

She just sat there grinning at me. We decided to call it a night and went to our bedroom to quietly fool around. Jessie was given a bottle of water and a box of crackers to prevent late night raids, and there was a bathroom just off her room so she didn't need to come down by our room.

We cuddled and were asleep quickly.

One o'clock in the morning, Lou Grossman was sitting quietly at his desk in the dark with only the desk lamp lighting his computer and didn't hear the man enter his room. Lou was a reporter for the Vegas Sun newspaper and was trying to make a morning deadline for his article about the vigilante. He had about two hours to email the copy to make the press run for the Sunday paper, if his editor even approved it. He didn't have much to go on because he knew so little about the Vegas Vigilante other than what his sources in the police department passed on to him, which wasn't much. He figured he would just wing it.

Lou heard a noise behind him and turned to see the shadow of someone in the dark of his room. He was startled and grabbed a long neck beer bottle from his desk, holding it by the neck and ready to bash the head of his intruder.

"Don't worry Lou. I'm not going to hurt you," the dark figure said. "I'm going to give you a story so you may want to get a pad and take notes."

"Who are you?"

"I'm the Vegas Vigilante, Lou. You may have heard of me."

"Yeah, I was just writing about you for tomorrow's paper. You said you have a story?" Lou didn't feel threatened by the man since he only killed abusers and Lou never struck anyone in his life.

"Get your pad. I don't have a lot of time. That is, if you want a lead story for the front page complete with your by-line."

Lou spun in his chair, grabbed the yellow legal pad and a pencil from his desk, and turned back to the figure still in the shadows. Lou could almost see the man's features, but he was masked.

Lou brought out a pocket recorder, but the man said not to record his voice, so Lou set the device down and took the pad to his lap. "I'm ready then."

"Good. Now I want to explain that I'm not a murderer. I'm a mercy killer for the helpless and I execute only those persons who abuse women and children."

For the next half hour the vigilante spoke of his purpose as Lou scribbled furiously.

**

Chapter 16

I would have liked to take my Sunday off, but I had told Deacon I would help him, and when he called me at 6:30, I had to say I'd come in. He told me Captain Weber woke him at 6 a.m. and said that he was assigning more men to the vigilante case under Deacon's command and wanted results fast. He was getting heat from the city council to solve this. Murder is never good for Sin City, just gambling and hookers.

I sat on the edge of the bed and felt my body slowly cracking itself back into position. I did a few leg lifts, knee bends, and that was my exercise for the morning. I turned to the bed where Penny was still asleep. She was so quiet, I hoped she was all right. Then she spoke.

"Sweetie, can you catch this guy so we can spend our weekends together? I think Jessie needs a father figure and you are becoming an absentee father." I could hear Penny speaking from under her pillow.

"Let's not get too attached to Jessie. Warren is still looking for relatives and she may be leaving us anytime. I like her, and she is good company for you, but she can't stay with us old people."

"I've known people who were raised by their grandparents. They turned out all right," she said, pulling the pillow from her head.

Vegas Vigilante Murders

"We're not grandparents, thank you."

"You are. You have a grandson back in Michigan."

"Okay, technicality, but we are not Jessie's grandparents. If Warren can't find any relatives, we have to decide what to do and I don't like the idea of dropping her in a foster home. Think about it while I go fight crime. Where's my cape and mask?"

Penny giggled. "Next to your tights, Super Gramps."

I smacked her on the butt as she rolled over in the bed. She said, "Be careful, the vigilante may get you for abuse."

I dressed, fed Willy, had my toast and was out the door after saying good morning to Jessie as she came out from the hallway followed by Penny. Driving to Metro was pleasant that morning, no traffic to make the trip a pain. I arrived and saw Deacon standing outside talking to Warren.

Deacon was holding a newspaper and looking rather pissed. "Good morning to the both of you," I said.

Deacon held out the copy of the Vegas Sun to me. On the front page blared the headline, "Vigilante Speaks!" in 120 point Helvetica bold.

I took the paper and glanced at the copy. It was pretty much what I figured the vigilante would say to cover his butt. Now he was trying for sainthood.

"I presume this is something you weren't expecting?" I asked.

"I should send a man to pick up this reporter,

Grossman, so we can question him. Nice he talked to the vigilante and didn't call the police. I'm going to see if we can hold him for accessory after the fact. Shithead is just stirring up trouble for a by-line."

I was still reading and said, "He says he couldn't see the vigilante, that he kept himself hidden. But he doesn't say he was using crutches."

"Yeah, well, we can totally rule the doc out. Now we have to take a different attack on this. At least we had no murders this morning."

Deacon's cell phone rang and he looked at the caller ID. It was Metro. "Crap, the captain probably has seen the paper by now." He answered the phone, bracing for loud yelling, listened for a few beats then hung up. "Hell, I spoke too soon. This just keeps getting better. We had another killing out in your neck of the woods this morning. The vigilante strikes again," Deacon said to me.

This was something new. I wasn't worried about Penny since this guy wasn't a random serial killer. He had specific goals in his murders. Deacon told Warren to get on the voice call from the TV station and see what they had at the lab. He went off and Deacon turned to me. "Shall we go see what new direction this case is taking?"

Deacon didn't even pull a car from the motor pool. We took his Vibe, or I should say Lynn's Vibe, and drove out toward my home. We were about two miles from my address and pulled up to a secluded house off the road. The place was a mess with weeds growing wild everywhere between the rocks of the desert landscaping that was poorly tended. The house needed painting badly and the screens were sitting against the house as though someone had forgotten to put them up.

We walked to the front door, passing the uniformed cops and yellow tape and found ME Joe Lang already there. We went through the screen door and were just inside the door when we saw Joe kneeling over the body. "Talk to me, Joe," Deacon said.

"The victim, Mark Sottero, was stabbed about twenty to thirty times. I'm having trouble counting them. He was stabbed in the back and the front. Looks like the vigilante turned him over to hack at him."

"Do we know it was the vigilante?" I asked.

Lang pointed towards a woman sitting in the other room. "Talk to the wife."

Deacon went in and told the officer watching the woman that he would take it. The cop nodded and stood back while Deacon sat on the couch next to the woman. She was plain looking with drab clothing and hair pulled back in a bun. The most noticeable thing about her was the bruises and cuts on her face and neck.

"Mrs. Sottero, I'm Detective DeAngelo. I know this is not a good time for you but we need to get on this quickly to catch the killer. Can you tell me what happened?"

She was in a daze and looked at Deacon, just staring. "He was beating on me. He did that a lot. He was a mean man. I was on the couch here taking his abuse when someone came through the front door, busting the glass. A man in black walked into the room, came up to Mark and grabbed his hair. I told Mark that long hair would be his downfall. The man dragged Mark out in the hallway where I couldn't see. I could hear screaming and banging on the floor, then it got quiet. I went to find him on the floor, bleeding. I called 911 and just sat here till they came." Her voice trailed off.

I could see she had no blood spatter on her so it was a good bet she didn't do it. Deacon asked, "Did the man leave right after the stabbing?"

"Yes, it was over quickly. I didn't see where the man went to. We are so secluded out here, I didn't even hear a car. He just vanished into thin air."

The EMS unit had arrived and Deacon let the EMTs check the woman. We went back out to the hallway. Lang's men were putting the body in the bag. CSI had finished their investigation and Deacon asked for a quick evaluation. He added that this was a priority now per Captain Weber.

Deacon bent over one of the EMTs on his knees treating the woman and asked, "Ma'am, can you describe the man to me?"

She looked up at him as the man was dressing her wounds. "He was as tall as Mark. They stood together so I could see that. He had on all black and a vest like the ones you see in the cop shows. Yes, the SWAT people wear them. He had a black hood on. It was tucked into his collar and there were holes cut so he could see."

"I know it's a stretch, but did you notice the color of his eyes?"

"Yes, as a matter of fact I did. When he grabbed Mark, he looked at me. He had odd eyes, light colored almost yellow-like. It was odd."

"Thank you, ma'am. These men will take you in to LV Medical to be checked to be sure you weren't injured worse."

She looked at Deacon and said quietly, "I hope he gets away."

Deacon turned out of the room. I kept up. "The guy is definitely becoming a folk hero," he said.

Deacon asked me to follow him and we went outside. He stood in the middle of the front yard surveying the property and said, "Now where would he go off to if he had no car? If he had a car, there isn't a lot of area to park a car for a quick getaway. There are no neighbors near enough to have seen anything. The wife said she heard no car. I wonder what vehicle he could have used."

"Bicycle?" I smiled.

"That would be quiet enough, but not much of a getaway vehicle." We walked around the house and found the property next door was a big vacant lot full of dirt, rocks and cactus. It went on for as far as we could see. Deacon walked to the edge of the property and then walked the length of the lot. He stopped at the back of the property when he saw what looked like tracks in the dirt, a single line of tire tracks. "Motorcycle or dirt bike," he said quietly. We walked out, following the tracks for a while until the desert area came up to a back road going to the hills on the left and the city on the right. "Well, we know how he got away." He pulled his cell phone, called dispatch, and said to put out a BOLO for any kind of motorcycle being ridden by a man in all black, most likely splattered in blood.

I laughed and said, "That could be most of the bikers in North Vegas."

**

Chapter 17

We went back to the house and found Sottero being escorted to the EMS unit. Deacon came up and stopped them, asking, "Mrs. Sottero, just one last question. Did you go to the 6th Street clinic for any treatments in the last six months?"

"No, I didn't. I've only gone to University Medical Center for anything needing attention."

"Do you know a Doctor Winston, Steve Winston?"

"No, the name's not familiar."

"What was the name of your physician?"

"Dr. Frank Carlson."

"Thank you, ma'am, I hope you'll get better."

They helped her up into the vehicle and then drove off. Deacon was standing with his arms folded across his massive chest and said quietly, "We need to get some leads. I hope forensics can find something to give us a clue."

"Frank Carlson treated her. Shall we look into his client list?"

"We'd have to get a warrant and go through the same crap we did with 6th Street. I wish Lynn was here."

"Don't go lame on me now, Deacon. You can do this. You're just too used to goofing off while Lynn does the work."

"Yeah, and I enjoyed it," he said with a grin.

The supervisor of the CSI was coming out of the house. Deacon went to him. "Larry, we found some tire tracks from a motorcycle or dirt bike at the back corner of the property. Can you have someone make impressions? It could be the vehicle the killer used to get away."

"Sure, Deacon, I'll have someone on it. Thanks. We didn't get much in the house. This guy was in and out too quickly to leave any trace. You got a mystery on your hands." He went back, yelling for his people.

"Yep, it's a mystery," Deacon said.

~~*~~

The masked man removed his hood and stood looking at his reflection in the bathroom mirror. He needed a shave badly, but he wasn't working at his job for now and didn't need to impress anyone. A voice came from the hallway, "Hey, how'd it go?"

"Quick and painless... for me. The guy was just a waste of life. Any kid could have done the job. We're treading on thin ice here, a kill each day. We need to be careful."

"No one is going to find us. Just be careful and fast, like you have been. I wish I could help, but you know I'll supply you with the victims so I guess I'm part of the team." He laughed and said, "Team

110

Vigilante! I like that. We strike fear into the hearts of lowlifes everywhere. In another few days Vegas will know not to abuse people. Fear will strike in their hearts. We will have won a small victory. Come on, cheer up. You look too depressed."

"I'm not supposed to be killing people. I'm supposed to be saving lives, not taking them."

"You're taking lives that were not meant to live. Striking a blow for Kaylie. Don't forget that. That's our destiny now."

"Yeah, I just need to get my head into it. Who's next?"

"We're changing directions now, throwing something new into the mix. You'll like this one."

~~*~~

I sat in Lynn's office staring out into the squad room as Deacon talked to a couple detectives I didn't know. There were a good number of police in Vegas since it is a big city with so much potential for crime. They had to be covered. He wasn't smiling. I didn't like to see Deacon in a bad mood, but I knew he was serious about catching the vigilante. He finished and came back to the office.

"Forensics wants to see me. Shall we go?"

We walked around the building to a glass door opening to many people moving around in their respective labs, each doing their scientific best to help crack a case. The CSIs in this area were all law enforcement people but they were scientist first and officers second. Deacon led me to an office of the CSI supervisor, Larry Hanks.

"Hey, Larry, get any good imprints off the motorcycle?"

"Yes, we just got a hit on the make. It's a brand of tire used on Suzuki trail bikes. There are about three dealers in the city who carry that make. Do you want the list?"

"Sure, it's something to follow for now. Anything else to go on?"

"Well, the powder on the body of Bert Frasher turned out to be latex glove powder, the kind to make it easy to put on the gloves. Only a few manufacturers still use that powder. Most stopped because of rashes the powder caused in too many cases. Environmental allergies, people allergic to everything from perfume to cleaners. This powder is from a batch of gloves used by either medical or for sterile room conditions, like an electronic processing company."

"Medical, like in a clinic?"

"Sure they would use them, but not in hospitals. They are going more to non-latex nitrile gloves due to allergic reactions to latex. But you can still buy the latex gloves in any drugstore, with and without powder."

"Thanks for that. Anything else?"

"Yeah, I have a doctor friend at Valley View Hospital and he says the number of abuse victims has dropped in the last few days. Maybe this guy is doing a service."

112

"Don't you start putting him on a pedestal. He's still a murderer."

"Yeah, I guess so. Well good luck, that's all I have. This guy is good, clean and quick."

We went back to Lynn's office and Deacon was studying the list of motorcycle shops. He called to Warren in the squad room.

"Yeah, Deacon?"

"Take this list, find Williams and the two of you go check out these places for owners of Suzuki trail bikes. The getaway vehicle may have been this bike. Then cross-reference the owners to anyone in our investigations so far."

"Will do," Warren said and went off.

"Is Williams still a pain in the ass?" I asked.

"Yep, we give him the jobs that take most the day to do just to get him away from us." Deacon laughed.

A uniformed officer came to the door. "Deacon, we just got a call from a person who says they were almost run off the road by a man on a motorcycle wearing a black hood instead of a helmet. Could be the vigilante?"

"Is he still on the phone or did he leave a number?"

"I got his address." He handed a slip of paper to him and went off.

He turned to me. "Shall we go see this guy? It's something."

We left the building, took a car from the motor pool again, and drove to the person's home. Deacon knocked on the front door of the apartment and waited. The door opened and there stood an older gentleman in a robe. He looked like he was getting ready for bed or a bath.

"Yes, can I help you?"

Deacon flashed his badge, identified us and asked, "You made a call earlier that you were almost run off the road by someone on a motorcycle?"

"Yeah, the freak came roaring out of a side street almost in front of my car. I swerved to miss him and he flew down the road. I gave chase to kick the crap out of him but he did some good maneuvers to get away."

"Where did this happen?"

"I was going south on Jones Boulevard and he came out of Washington Avenue heading east. I followed him until about Rancho Drive. He turned south and I lost him at the light."

"What time was this?"

"About 8:30. I was listening to the news on the radio when he came at me."

"You reported he wasn't wearing a helmet but a black hood."

"Yes, he looked like one of those guys with the big ax who chops your head on the block."

"An executioner?"

"Yes, that's the guy. Is he a bad man?"

"He may be. Can you describe the motorcycle?"

"It was small, red and black and it was quiet. I never heard it go by me. It was one of those small motorcycles."

"Was it a dirt bike?"

"Don't know the difference, but it was small."

"I don't suppose you got the license plate number?"

"Nope, didn't see it. He was moving too quickly, like the devil was chasing him."

Deacon looked at me. I had nothing to ask. He thanked the man and we went back to the car.

"Well, it fits the approximate time. He was coming from the area of the crime and was on a dirt bike. I'm surprised a patrol car didn't pick up on him, being I put out the BOLO."

"Can you get something off the intersection cameras?" I asked.

"Yeah, if we can find the point where the old man nearly ran him down, maybe we can follow him to his destination. We need to go see the traffic controllers."

We got in the car and drove over to the building that housed the people who controlled and watched the flow of traffic using cameras on almost every corner. This city was surveillance heaven or hell depending on which side of the law you were on. We went in and Deacon found the supervisor of the shift. He showed his badge and said, "We need to find a dirt bike on Rancho Drive heading south around 8:30. Do you think you can help us?"

"We can try. Come on over."

The man went to a wall of monitors above a bank of keyboards. He asked a tech to move and sat at the controls. He did a lot of typing, and the screen in front of him ran in reverse very fast until the counter in the corner came to around 8:30, then the image slowed. The man did a few more enhancements and pulled back so we could see the whole intersection. He started the forward motion as we watched the screen.

"There he is," Deacon said, pointing to a dirt bike on the screen. "Can you follow him from there?"

The man was doing more typing as the screen changed points of view and we watched his back. The operator kept the image on the man for about three minutes as the man turned onto Sahara Avenue and over to the Sahara Hotel. The rider drove into the parking structure and that was it.

Deacon said, "Well, we know where he went. Shall we go see if we can find a motorcycle?"

**

Chapter 18

On the way to the Sahara Hotel Deacon called Warren and said to meet him there at the entrance to the parking structure. We arrived shortly after and found him waiting with Williams. We parked off on the side usually reserved for limos and recreational vehicles and met with the men.

"Did you have any luck with the dirt bike sales?" Deacon asked.

"We got a short list of Suzuki owners, but haven't had a chance to check them out."

"That's okay. We got a good lead on the bike. It may be parked in this place so we need to do a search to see if it's still here. Take the lower three levels and look for a dirt bike. Jim and I will take the levels above. Call if you spot anything."

Warren and Williams went off to their car and into the structure as Deacon and I went to our car to drive up to the levels that would take a while to search. The parking structure was huge.

On the way up I asked, "Why would the killer drive all the way to this place still wearing his mask? Why not change into a helmet?"

"One of the universe's mysteries. I thought about it too, but have no idea why. He may have felt superior wearing it or wanted to be caught."

"If so, he could have just driven through Metro's parking lot. I'm not seeing it. There are cameras on each level of this thing. His image could have been caught here too."

"We can check that after we see if he left the bike here. He may have had a car waiting to switch with."

"There's only one way up and down in this place so he should have to show up on surveillance by the exits," I said.

We arrived on the fourth level and drove around the parking spaces watching for the bike. We had finally reached the rooftop level and found a Suzuki dirt bike parked behind the rooftop edifice for the elevators. We exited the car and went to it.

"It's been ridden through dirt recently judging by the tires," Deacon said.

I went to the short retaining wall of the rooftop and looked down at the busy Las Vegas Boulevard passing in front of the building. From the roof I could see up the north end and down the south all along the strip. It was a sight that always thrilled me. Deacon was on his phone calling Warren and then called for CSI to come get the bike.

I looked around. The rooftop cameras were angled to show the front of the entrance for the elevators, but the bike was on the back of the small structure. "The vigilante could have parked, been picked up by someone and driven off or had a car up here to use. I guess the video will tell."

Warren and Williams arrived and Deacon told them to wait for CSI, that we were going to check with security. We drove back down, parked on the lower level and went into the building. We found a security person by the entrance to the hotel. Deacon showed his badge and asked if the man could take us to the security office. We went into the belly of the building and to the room containing the spy system of the hotel and casino. We met with the supervisor and Deacon explained the situation.

"You're saying we had the vigilante use our parking? That's not something we need to promote, not the image we need," he said. "What can I do for you?"

Deacon explained the time frame of the man driving his bike to the hotel parking. The supervisor went to his control panel and ran the video of the time in question. We watched as the vigilante drove his bike into the structure and then up to the roof where he went out of camera sight behind the elevators. We watched waiting for him to come around but didn't see any movement. The supervisor ran the video in fast forward, but still no movement.

I was trying to remember the layout of the roof and thought that the vigilante could have walked directly away from the elevators and over the side of the building. I told Deacon this and he said we'd check that shortly. I could see the live camera on the roof. CSI had arrived and was checking the bike.

Deacon thanked the man and we went back to our car. Driving back up, I said, "If he went over the side, he'd have to have all his gear set up before hand, ropes and such. He'd have to know what to expect up here."

"I'm wondering if he's acting alone. This is sounding to me like a lot of work for one person," Deacon said.

We arrived back up top and Deacon went to the lead CSI. He turned as Deacon came up and said, "We ran the VIN of the bike and it came up as stolen this morning from a home over off Desert Inn Road. We'll take it in and try to get some prints off it, but I'm sure the vigilante was wearing gloves. I'll let you know."

I said, "Could be a reason for the vigilante not having a helmet. If he stole it, the helmet may not have been with the bike."

Deacon walked to the edge of the roof behind the elevators. We looked over and could see the roof of the casino just below about six feet down. "The guy could have jumped to that roof and over to the back."

Deacon sat up on the ledge and swung his legs over. I knew what he had in mind. "I'm not interested in playing Spiderman. Give me the keys and I'll drive the car back down." He pulled out the keys and handed them to me saying I was getting old.

"Better believe it. I don't need to break any bones now." Deacon laughed, then jumped and headed to the back of the building as I went to the car and drove down.

I pulled out of the exit and turned towards where I thought Deacon would come down. I found a back alley of the building and there was Deacon looking around. I pulled up and parked, got out and joined him.

"It wasn't very hard to get down here this way. The vigilante would have had to use this route to escape. There's no parking back here, so he had to be picked up. Probably left his mask on so he wouldn't be identified if anyone saw him or he was caught on a camera."

"I don't see any cameras here so it was a safe place to be picked up. This is really a lot of work to avoid being seen—parking, jumping and being picked up," I said.

"Well, he wanted to be sure no one would follow him, and he succeeded. Unless the lab gets something, we are back to square one. Let's go talk to the employees and see if anyone saw something." He called Warren and told him to go to the employee dining room and ask if anyone saw a masked man around the back of the building. We got back in the car and drove to valet parking at the front entrance, parked and talked to the valet attendants. We didn't get anything worthwhile. We left and went back to Metro after Deacon called and asked if Warren had anything. He didn't. He told Warren to go back to security and see if he could spot any vehicles moving from the building around the time the vigilante would have escaped.

We arrived back at Metro and went in. Captain Weber was standing in the squad room. Deacon told me to wait in Lynn's office and went to Weber. The captain said, "I want a full report. Let's go to my office." Deacon looked sick and followed the captain.

I just sat in the office wondering what Penny was up to. I figured I would have the time and called.

"Hey, babe, how's your day so far?" I asked.

"Jessie, Willy and I are at the Boulevard Mall spending my hard earned money." She laughed. "We're just getting some things for Jessie's room, getting it decorated."

"Well, as I said, don't get too settled in with her. We still don't know what will happen yet. She may be leaving us soon."

"I know but this is fun and it's getting her mind off the tragedy of this week."

"That's a good thing. Have fun. There's not much to say about my activities. We're getting nowhere so far. I'll tell you more about it when I get home. Say hi to Jessie for me." She said she would and hung up. I sat back hoping Deacon survived Captain Weber.

The motel room was dingy and dark. The woman sat on the bed half dressed, her pimp standing in front of her, yelling in her face.

"Damn you, bitch, you must be holding out on

me. This isn't money like you should be making. I don't need to come here and find you sitting on your boney ass and not have a john between your skinny legs. What's the deal?"

The woman gave him a frightened look. "I haven't been feeling well, Luther. I got cramps something fierce," she wailed.

"I'll give you cramps, cramps to make you double over in pain if you don't start doing your job."

"I'm trying, Luther. Give me a day to get better."

"I ain't got no days to wait. Get out there and start hustling, bitch." He smacked her hard. She fell back. "Get your skank ass back out on the streets or I'll feed you more of that!" He raised his hand again. She shrank back. He gave her a grin and swung, just missing her.

The pimp went to the door, pulling it open, expecting to go into the hallway, but found a masked man all dressed in black. It was the last thing he saw.

**

Chapter 19

The call on Deacon's phone interrupted Captain Weber's lecture on finding the killer. Deacon listened and said to the captain, "We got another one. Vigilante is now killing pimps. Sorry, but I got to go. We can continue later." He went out and pulled me from the office. We went out the back door to the parking lot quickly, Deacon hoping to get away from the captain.

"What's up?" I asked.

"Got a fresh kill. A pimp was murdered in front of one of his women by a masked man in black. He's changing directions now, going after the lowlifes of prostitution, the pimps."

"There's going to be a field day for the media when they get a whiff of this."

"If this is our vigilante, I'm hoping it's not a copycat killing. We haven't had any response from the killer about going after pimps now. Anyone can put on a mask and go after anyone they want. This is the first kill that happened in the daylight also. All the others were done under cover of darkness so it makes me wonder."

We drove the rest of the way lost in our own thoughts and arrived at the motel off Bridger, two streets south from Fremont Street. We pulled in finding two cruisers and CSI already there. We went into the building and then were led by a uniform cop to the hallway where we found the room.

"Hey, Larry, busy day, huh?" Deacon said to the lead CSI.

"You better find this guy soon. Our budget is filling for overtime," he said. "You know they'll be complaining."

"Yeah, well, the bookkeepers can go after the criminals then. I was told there was a witness."

"Yeah, she's inside. They had to hold her down. She was bouncing all over the place, screaming about the murder."

"Thanks, Larry." Deacon went in. I stood at the door opening waiting to be allowed in the room by

Vegas Vigilante Murders

CSI. Larry looked at me and said it was all right, they had cleared the room. I came over to where the young black woman was on the bed crying her eyes out. Deacon was trying to get her to pay attention but she just kept rocking back and forth, wailing. Finally Deacon yelled in her face loudly, "Shut the fuck up".

She jerked her head up and went silent. Deacon said, "That's better. Now I want to know what happened here. Talk to me."

She wiped her eyes with a tissue and took a breath, saying, "I was discussing with Wolfie about business and he went to the door, opened it and there stood this guy all in black and with a mask. He done grabbed Wolfie by the throat and walked his ass back in the room, kicking the door closed with his foot. He then lifted Wolfie off the floor by his throat. That man was strong! Wolfie was flailing around like a rag doll and then the man threw Wolfie against the wall and while Wolfie was on the ground the man grabbed his head and just spun it. Wolfie's head just snapped and he be dead. The man looked at me and put his finger to his face like he wanted me to be quiet, so I was. He turned and went out of the room. I just sat not believing what I had witnessed. In all my life I never had seen such a sight. May I go to the bathroom? I got cramps something fierce."

Deacon told her to go ahead but not be in there all day. She ran to the room and closed the door. Deacon came to me and said, "She said something that came up before. I think the young girl Noel said that about the killer making the quiet sign with his finger to his mouth area. I'm thinking this is our man.

Well, do we have to pull in all the pimps in town to protect them now?"

"It might make it easier on the girls if you did." I grinned. "Or better yet, leave them out there and let this guy clean up the town."

"Don't you start. I'm supposed to keep people alive, not let them get murdered even if they are criminals." Warren came in as we were talking and Deacon asked, "Did you get anything on the surveillance videos?"

"We watched back and forth for about an hour of video. There were just too many cars coming and going around the back. Can't tell which one picked up our bad guy."

"Okay, you and Williams go room to room questioning if anyone saw or heard anything."

"I hate talking to transients. They never cooperate," he said gloomily as he went back out.

"Speaking of transients, how did the vigilante know where to go and how did he slip by everyone without being seen?" I asked.

"Maybe he has a look-out. The vigilante could have been hiding in a car or van and when his spy found out where the kill was to take place, he alerted the killer."

"Wow, you are getting the hang of this deducting, aren't you?"

"I've been taking a course by mail." He smiled. We stood waiting for the woman to come back out.

Warren came back to the door and called us out. "I got a witness who saw the man in black get into a dark blue van out back being driven by another man.

Vegas Vigilante Murders

He was wearing a hat so the wit says he couldn't see his face too well. I got a description of the van and called a BOLO already."

"Thanks, Greg. Maybe they didn't get far enough away." He turned to me and said, "There are two of them. This is getting interesting."

"One committing the murders and one doing the leg work of finding the victims? Tag team killings maybe. Either way, this is two kills in one day. He or they are escalating."

~~*~~

The men had just dumped the van behind a vacant building off Fremont and Eastern Avenue. It would take days before anyone would find the van and they had wiped it clean. They got into the Toyota Celica and drove out onto Eastern. The vigilante had pulled his mask off and sat back in the seat.

"I know that old man saw us. I'm sure he will tell the cops, but we were quick enough to get away and dump the van. We are getting too confident with this kill. It's too soon after the one this morning. We have to back off."

"No, we need to strike while the iron is hot, as they say. All this is going to make people pay attention to our cause. The pimps and abusers will tremble with fear from us. We need to make another statement for this kill. I'll call the TV people again and let them know we mean business."

"You realize the old man will tell the cops he saw two people. We now are no longer the lone vigilante."

"Yes, but that makes us all the stronger now, two people to worry about. I'll announce that we are a team of assassins bent on wreaking havoc in Vegas. Scum beware!"

"You know sometimes you even frighten me. You're taking this seriously, aren't you?"

"And you don't think murder is serious? We made a pact to take out these people. Let's not forget that."

~~*~~

The hooker came out of the bathroom. Deacon told Warren to take her in and question her until she had her facts straight, take her statement, then cut her loose.

Deacon and I drove back to Metro and he dropped off the unmarked car. It was getting late and we were both weary so we stopped for the day. Or at least I did. Crime didn't stop for Deacon. I knew he was going back in to finish his talk with Weber, and I felt for him. With luck, Weber had already signed out for the day and Deacon would get a reprieve for the night.

"I'll see you tomorrow. Just try not to make it too early." I laughed.

"I don't plan on starting too early myself but crime has a way of rousting me out of bed. I'll try not to disturb you if I can. I'll make it up to you one day.

I just need your extra push to help me." He saluted me and turned away.

Deacon went back into Metro and I went to my car. I meant to ask him if he had heard from Lynn lately and was filling her in on the case. Probably not. She would be having fits knowing what was going on. She wasn't scheduled to be back for three weeks. Hopefully the case would be solved by then, if it even got solved. I drove out to the house and found Penny's car still in the drive. I wondered what they had purchased at the mall. I hoped Penny wasn't getting Jessie too settled in with us. I liked the girl and we probably could take care of her, but our lives were a bit hectic to think of raising a pre-teenager. I realized I didn't even know when her birthday was. Some father I was. I laughed to myself when I thought that.

I pulled into the garage, stood looking at my twenty-three year old Crown Vic, smiling that it still looked good and went into the house, finding it quiet. I heard a small amount of noise from back by the bedrooms and then heard a loud screeching noise emanating from Jessie's room. I had my hand on my Glock and walked carefully down the hall. I came to the door and the noise was worse, screaming and howls. I peeked around the doorframe and saw Penny, Willy and Jessie doing some kind of gyrating moves. I laughed. They were dancing to a music CD.

**

Chapter 20

I moved into the door opening and stood watching them dance around the room. Penny suddenly saw me and waved, but kept on dancing. Jessie saw Penny wave and looked at me, smiled and yelled, "We're practicing for Dancing with the Stars."

I yelled to have fun and went out to the kitchen. Again, I hadn't eaten while I was out. I might lose some weight at this rate. Willy came trotting in and was wagging his tail for me. I reached down and petted him. "I suppose you haven't been fed either." He yipped once.

Penny came in and told me not to make anything to eat, we were going out to eat, her treat. I just grinned and asked, "Do I get to pick the place?"

"No, we're going to a new restaurant in Neonopolis at Fremont. I've heard good things about it. Now go get cleaned up. You smell of crime."

"Yes, dear," I said and went to obey her.

We piled into the car, drove over to Fremont Street, and parked in the Golden Nugget parking structure. We walked through the plaza as the overhead video was presenting its show. We got to the restaurant and they had a good selection of foods from around the world. I chose good old hamburgers and onion rings from the United States.

We had our fill of food and the girls babbled on about their trip to the mall, telling me about all the good things they bought. Penny asked me about my

129

day. I said I'd tell her later, that it wasn't decent dinner talk.

We wandered around the Fremont Street plaza again and took in all the sights and the millions of flashing lights. Even though I had seen them many times, they still fascinated me. We headed back and I reminded Penny and Jessie that she would need to go register for school the next day. Jessie made a disappointed noise but said she'd look forward to it. Penny said we needed to go buy school supplies. She really loved shopping. We stopped at Wal-Mart and picked up the basics for school. To Penny that meant filling a cart.

We arrived back home and went in to relax.

~~*~~

Around 4 A.M. the man in the black mask was hiding behind bushes on the side of a motel that was frequented by hookers off the strip. He waited for the right minute as he watched the woman with her pimp arguing about something sexual. The two of them were walking towards a room, passing the bushes, when the masked man jumped out and attacked the pimp. The woman screamed and started bashing the masked man with her bag. The pimp was fairly agile. He held off the man and then connected a good punch to the masked man's face. The man fell back as the woman ran to the motel office and was screaming for the police. The pimp held the masked man down until the first patrol car pulled up and took the man from the pimp.

Bob Moats

Deacon was awakened from a good sleep, listened to the voice on the phone then jumped out of bed to get dressed. He was excited. They had caught the vigilante.

~~*~~

I got out of bed early and was getting ready for the day when the call came in. Deacon was yelling that they caught him. I was glad but said I had to take care of getting Jessie in school that morning so he'd have to handle it by himself, but I'd be in later.

Deacon hung up his phone, turned to Warren who was looking miserable from lack of sleep, and said, "Let's go see our killer."

They walked down to interrogation and Deacon was told by a uniformed officer that the perp was in room 3. Deacon and Warren went into observation and stood at the mirror, looking at the man sitting quietly at the table. He had on black jeans and a black leather jacket. His mask was off and he looked like some weasel off the street.

"Damn, this guy doesn't impress me for being the killer who took out a couple big men with just a twist of their heads, and his outfit is wrong. Do we have an ID on him yet?" he asked the uniform.

The cop held out a sheet to Deacon and said, "He came up as Louie Grayson, small time hood and wannabe pimp. He's been pulled in a couple times for starting fights with other pimps. I hate to say it but I don't think he's our guy."

131

Vegas Vigilante Murders

Deacon's body slumped as he stared at the wretch in the other room. "Damn! We're getting copycats now. Well, let's go see what he has to say." Deacon left observation followed by Warren and the uniform.

They burst into the room causing Grayson to jump. Deacon pulled the chair out, sat hard and leaned on the table, looking at Grayson with a snarl. "Who the hell do you think you are? You were masquerading as the vigilante and it almost got you killed. Why?"

Grayson sat quietly. His eyes were droopy and red, probably from drugs. He looked at Deacon and said, "I want my lawyer."

"Do you have a lawyer or do we call in a public defender? You know you were caught in the act, attacking a man. A lawyer is just going to laugh at you. Still want one?"

"I got nothing to say."

Deacon turned to the uniform and asked, "Has he been processed yet?"

The cop said he was and then Deacon said, "Put him in a cell with a few other pimps and let him stew."

The man's eyes went big and he wailed, "You do that and if they think I'm the vigilante, I'll get the shit kicked out of me. Hey, I need protection here."

"Well, tell that to your lawyer, if we can find one in time."

"Okay, what do you want? I'm not the vigilante!"

"I didn't think you were. You aren't good

132

enough to carry his mask. What were you trying to accomplish?"

"I wanted to take over Morgan's territory. I thought if I scared him he'd move out."

"What if the real vigilante found you out prancing around in your mask? You think he would have just scared you?"

Grayson went silent. He was rolling his head around thinking about what Deacon had said. "I guess I didn't think it out too well."

"Yeah, you didn't." He turned to the uniform and said to book him for aggravated assault and find a hole to put him it. Deacon stood and went out.

"Crap, I thought it was over. Any word so far as to a real attack by the vigilante?"

Warren said there had been no reports.

~~*~~

Penny and I finished at the school we were placing Jessie in. The principal took Jessie to her first class after she said she'd take care of the rest. Penny had to go her studio and said she'd pick up Jessie after school. I kissed her and drove over to Metro.

I found Deacon standing by a desk in the squad room. "So where's the killer?"

Deacon gave me a pained look and said, "He's a copycat, couldn't do any damage to an old lady if he tried. We haven't had any reports of attacks by the real vigilante yet, just waiting for something. I wish this guy would leave some trace so we can get his trail."

Vegas Vigilante Murders

"Well, if you need me, call. I should go to my office to see if it's still there. I'll talk later."

Deacon took a sip from his coffee mug, made a face and said he'd see me later. I went back out to my car, disappointed that they hadn't caught him. I drove over to my office and pulled into the parking out front. I entered and saw Lacey smiling at me. "Good morning stranger. We missed you."

"I'm sure you didn't miss me over the weekend. How's the place doing?"

"Quiet. Buck is in his office with Mac going over schedules and resolving problems at the gas stations. Guards are not happy with the quality of customers. They are all about ready to start shooting." She laughed.

"Yeah, well, I'd say go ahead and shoot but that wouldn't be right. It's Buck's job to tell them." I went to my office followed by Willy who was picked up by Lacey early that morning. I picked him up and put him on the chair next to me and he plopped down. Trapper came to my door, grinning.

"I picked up a client from Barnes, a friend. His wife may be cheating on him. I'm having him come in today to talk about it."

"Speaking of Barnes, how's his wife doing?"

"He called me this morning and said she was getting in a program for gambling and sex addiction and he was happy with our investigations. He's mailing a check for his payment. His wife said that she was thinking about the day she took Art Kramer to that room and she says she remembers a man following them. She thought he was maybe a P.I.

checking on her. She was suspicious of anyone tailing her. She may remember what he looked like. Could be your vigilante stalking Kramer."

I sat thinking about that. "Yeah, that's good. I'll call Alicia Barnes and talk to her. Thanks. Where's your case taking you?"

"Just down to Henderson, my first hometown, and the hubby thinks his wife is entertaining in his own house when he's at work. Should be easy enough."

"Why doesn't the husband just come home early and catch them?"

"He wants to have a P.I. to do the leg work so he can use it for a divorce. He says she's a bitch on wheels and he wants out of the marriage. He had a clause in the pre-nup that states if either party cheats, they forfeit all claims to property and cash. I get the goods and he gets the prize."

"I hope you asked for a percentage of his win." I laughed.

We heard the tinkle of the front door bell. Trapper turned and said his client was there. He went to greet him and I picked up the phone to call Alicia Barnes.

**

Vegas Vigilante Murders

Chapter 21

Chester Barnes answered the phone and I told him who I was. He thanked me again for our work in helping save Alicia. I asked if she was there. He said she was.

"I'm taking some time off from work to be with her for now. I'll get her." He put the phone down and I could hear him calling his wife. I waited.

"Hello," came a shaky voice.

"Mrs. Barnes, I'm Jim Richards. We haven't met but I own the private investigating firm your husband hired. I've heard that you may have seen a man following you and Arthur Kramer to the Flamingo. I'm sorry to bring this unpleasantness back up, but I'm helping the police track down the vigilante. Anything you can tell me would help."

"Mr. Richards, I'd be happy to help catch the killer, but I have to leave now for my therapy. Can we meet after?"

"That would be fine. You name the place and I'll meet you there."

"I'm going to be over at Maryland and Tropicana. Do you know the lounge in the Tropicana Hotel?"

"I'm familiar with it, yes."

"How about one o'clock?"

"Fine, I'll see you then." We finished up and I called Deacon.

"Hey, it's me. I may have a small lead for you.

Seems that Art Kramer's hook up that got him killed yielded a possible sighting of our killer. Alicia Barnes said she spotted a man tailing them to the hotel. I'm going to have a talk with her when she gets out of her gambling and sex addiction session. Want to tag along?"

"I'll let you take care of it. I'm going to be in a meeting all this afternoon with Weber. He thinks we need a plan, so we waste time listening to him plot the thing out. Let me know if you find out anything."

"Will do, have fun," I said and hung up after he finished saying good-bye. I checked my email and messages on the machine. Nothing earth shattering.

Buck came in and dropped into my client chair. "Jimmy, I'm befuddled. My guards are all starting to sound like old ladies. I know that crime is a fact of life uptown, but these guys signed on to protect and serve the clients. I don't want to see anyone get shot. That's why I have all my men go through a gun handling course so they'll know what to do in that situation. I thought I hired tough guys but they are starting to wimp out on me."

"No one wants to get shot for what these men are being paid. Not that you aren't being generous with your paydays, but it's hazardous out there. Offer a bounty of cash for every save they do, stopping a crime. Maybe that will give them incentive."

"Yeah, that might work. I just hope they don't start trouble to collect." He grinned and stood, said he'd talk later, and left the room.

I had seen Trapper and his client walk past my door, and then Mac went the other way towards

Lacey. I got up and walked out. Willy was sound asleep so I went quietly. I went to the lobby and found Mac talking to Lacey. He said hello.

"So when are you two going to get married? You keep talking about it."

Mac looked at Lacey and said, "When we have enough money saved to do it right." He gave me a big grin and Lacey just blushed.

"I'll tell you what. When you feel ready, I'll give you your wedding as a gift. It's something I couldn't do for my son when he got married, but I gave them a renewal of vows wedding last year to make up for it. But I'd like to do it up good from the start. It might be fun." I turned to Lacey. "Just don't turn into a Bridezilla. I had enough of that already," I said, referring to the Bridezilla murders I had suffered with already.

"Well, thank you, Jim. That's more than generous. We've been talking about it happening soon and will let you know when."

"Good, just don't make it too expensive, but have fun with it. I'm not Donald Trump."

They laughed and I said I had business to do and said to tell Buck and Trapper I was gone. I went back to my car, drove to the nearest Subway, and got a sub sandwich. I hadn't had fast food in a couple of days so I wanted to make up for it. I went to the Tropicana and into the lounge. I was early but I liked to get the lay of the land scoped out before meeting with Alicia.

I'd never seen her in person, but I had seen her picture so I knew what to expect. I sat and had a couple glasses of Pepsi. An attractive woman came in, it was her. I stood and waved to her. She came over.

"Mr. Richards, so good to meet you," she said.

I asked her to sit, and the waitress was over quickly. She ordered a Tom Collins. I asked for another Pepsi.

"You don't drink, Mr. Richards?"

"I'm a beer drinker, but not this early. I don't indulge until after eight at night."

"I like that in a man, dedication to principles." She had a smile on her face that was more than friendly. I hoped her sex addiction was kept in check.

"Can you tell me about the man you saw follow you in the hotel?" I said before she started anything.

"I saw him at O'Shea's casino first when I picked up Kramer, and then I saw him again in the Flamingo lobby, trying to be unobtrusive."

I was glad Trapper hid better. "What did he look like?"

"Short, a bit shorter than I am which would put him at about five-six. He had black hair, cut like a business person, styled well. He was ordinary, medium nose. I couldn't see his eyes. He had on narrow shades. That's how I saw him again, those shades. He was dressed in dark blue jeans and a pullover shirt like the golfers wear. Oh and one more thing, he had ears that stuck out like Howdy Doody. Do you remember Howdy Doody?"

"Showing my age, yes, I do. So they stuck out prominently?"

"Yes, they did. That man needs plastic surgery. He could fly with those ears."

139

"That's a big help. Could you give me your take on how he could have gotten in the room?"

"Well, Art did go to check the passage door to the next room to be sure it was locked but I watched him and I'm not sure if it was locked on our side when he closed the door. The killer could have come in that way."

"That would be very fortunate for the killer if the door was unlocked. I think he came in that way also, but he had to be able to unlock the door if it was locked. So it may not have mattered if Kramer had left it unlocked. How long were you in the room before taking the shower?"

"Well, he wasn't a slow lover. He rushed through it and about passed out. Not in good shape. I had to wash off his body odor and sweat. He reeked. I had to take care of it. I was going to sneak out after the shower, but came out and found him…" She paused, looking upset. "I found him dead. I freaked out and went to the hallway, screaming. I was panicking in the hall when security came."

"I'm sorry for your situation. It was bad, I'm sure. I'm trying to help a friend on the Vegas police catch this killer, and any help from you is welcome. Do you think you could come in to give a sketch artist your take on the face of the man?"

"If it would help to make me get over this incident, I'd be glad to."

"Great, let me make a call and we'll get you set up." I pulled my cell phone and called Deacon.

"Hi, Jim. I'm still in the meeting with Weber, but

your call is welcome. It got me out of the room for a moment. What's up?"

"I got a woman who may be able to give a description of the vigilante without his mask or maybe the other guy. Can you set up something with your sketch artist?"

"Sure, bring her in. I can get it set up for you, and it will get me away from Weber. Thank you."

I asked Alicia if she could go in now. She had nothing better to do. "Yeah, she can make it. Go ahead and we'll be in shortly." I hung up and then paid for her drink. She said she'd follow me. We went to Metro and in.

Deacon had the artist set up in a conference room and Alicia sat with him working on the portrait. I stood with Deacon outside the room watching her give the description. The man was drawing quickly.

"Weber wants a full out attack on the vigilante. I think he's getting heat from above. So far there have been no reports of murders today, but the day isn't over yet."

We went to sit in the squad room where we still could see Alicia and waited. About a half hour later, they stood and came out of the room. Deacon went to the artist and he showed Deacon the picture. It was a good rendering and might be helpful.

"So this is the face you remember following you?" Deacon asked.

"As sure as I can be. I got to see him twice and I was watching him. I don't think he knew I saw him."

"That's good. You shouldn't be in any danger." Deacon called to Warren and said, "Get this picture

141

out on the LEIN and to the media. We are going to shake his tree now."

**

Chapter 22

Deacon and I thanked Alicia and she went off to go home to her husband who was waiting for her. He had to stay home with their son who was ill that day.

"That's sad what that woman went through. With the gambling, sex and then the murder, I'm surprised she isn't in a mental hospital. Well, do you think this picture may help?"

"I hope so. It may get Weber off my back for now."

Warren came back and said to go to the TV in the break room. We did and Warren had it set to the news. The anchorperson was just sitting as the picture changed. "This is a new call to our station from the Vegas Vigilante received about twenty minutes ago. This time we received a video taken by the vigilante. It is not for the squeamish, and we've given a copy to the police." Deacon mumbled that they didn't give him any copy. "Listen carefully. Maybe you can recognize the voice or see something in the video you may know."

The screen cut away to the vigilante standing in what looked like a basement. He was in shadows but recognizable. He moved closer to the camera and spoke through his mask.

"People of Las Vegas, I am the Vigilante, and

I'm here to protect our citizens from the scourge that is making our streets unsafe to walk. The pimps who march their women on the streets where it is illegal to do their business will be given notice to cease and desist. The abusers of women and children have not been forgotten. I will be settling with them further, but now we have to punish the abusive pimps. This is what will happen to you if you keep up on the course you are going."

The man walked to the side as the camera followed. They had a man tied to a chair with a gag in his mouth. He looked terrified. The vigilante walked behind him, took hold of his head, and just before he twisted it, the scene cut away back to the newsperson.

"We've stopped this video due to the murder that was committed, not suitable for viewers. Our calls to the police have, of course, been given a no comment as of now. We will keep you informed as there are developments."

Deacon picked up a bottle of cola from the table and threw it at the screen. It was plastic so it didn't do any damage.

"Mother fuckers, they just love beating up the police, don't they? I'd like to see them find the killer! Do they think this is a damn picnic?" He stopped and took a big breath. Everyone in the room started to applaud him, then he stormed out.

Warren and I looked at each other. I shrugged and followed Deacon's lead. I saw him in the squad room picking up the artist sketch and then he was heading towards the front of the building. Warren came out after me and we went following Deacon who was moving quickly. Deacon burst through the front doors and stopped where the news crews were standing waiting for a bone.

Deacon held up his hand and yelled, "Okay, vultures, gather around." The men and women of the news ran forward, thrusting microphones towards Deacon who yelled to back off or he would shoot the first person who touched him. He had a look in his eyes as if he would. They weren't sure of his mental state and backed up.

"All right, cameras ready, I'm making a statement. To the media who have been more than unkind to us, I say we are working diligently to track down the vigilante. We aren't just sitting on our asses and playing chess. We want this man caught and are doing everything we can. If you can do better, do so, make my life easier. We have extended our personnel to include outside experts to help catch him. We have a witness who gave us an image of the possible vigilante." He was holding the sketch copy but waving it around so the cameras had a problem focusing on it. "We have distributed this sketch to the media, so you can drive people to help find the killer. We need your help, not criticism, so please do us a favor and stop making this a vendetta against the police. We are only capable of doing our job without the crap the news puts on us. So wise up, all of you, and help us, not be asses. No questions."

He stormed back into the station, ignoring the screams and yells of the reporters wanting a sound byte. I was standing just outside the entrance and went in followed by Warren.

"You'll probably catch hell from Weber, but I think you told it straight up," I said to Deacon after he stopped in Lynn's office to sit.

"Those people need to back off," he said as his desk phone rang. He answered and had a shocked look on his face. He signaled to Warren to track it. "What do you want?"

He put the call on speakerphone and leaned towards the box now giving out the voice. "Hey, Deacon, you are cool, and you tell it like it is. But you'll never catch me, not even if you do have a sketch of who you think is me. Now be a good boy and let me do my job. You can't get these criminals in and convict them. Let me do the justice you need."

Deacon spoke up. "Listen creep, I am the law. I bring in these criminals and do what I can to get them convicted."

The voice laughed. "What's your conviction rate? One conviction for every five arrests? You got shit, and you know it. Not your fault. The courts are so crammed and the judges and lawyers are stupid. They'll get theirs. I have a conviction rate of 100 percent. Let me do what I need to do. Back off now."

"Why are you doing this?"

The voice said, "I am avenging wrongs committed years ago to a defenseless woman that should never have happened. I am avenging those people who can't stand up for themselves and take control of the situation they are in. Life sucks and the bad guys win. I'm evening out the odds."

The call cut out. Warren came back in and said

the guy cut them off just a few seconds before they could get a fix. He knew the set-up.

Deacon sat back and said, "This guy was out there. He saw me. They had no time to broadcast my statement. Damn, he was here. He knows the routine. He has to be in the system. Someone who knows how the game works."

"Are you saying he's a cop, reporter or someone in the legal field?" I asked.

"Well, it sounds like that to me. I could be wrong, but I'm almost sure of this. He is in the system."

"He said he was avenging a wrong committed to a woman years ago. That ring a bell?"

"Hell, no. I don't remember every case we've had. I'll need to have some men run the cases and see how many we've had of abuse or murder of women or children involving cops, reporters or legal people. The pimp angle, I'm not sure of. He may just be hitting them to pump up his conviction rate. Damn." Deacon was incensed. I had never seen him so worked up, even back in Michigan when we worked on cases together.

"Warren, cross-reference past abuse murder cases with cops who may have been close to the victims. See what you can come up with." Warren said he would and went out of the room.

"Jim, I am so upset right now, I could scream." I had never seen Deacon so intent on a case. I hoped he didn't have a coronary.

"Have you talked to Lynn lately?" I asked, hoping it would change his mood.

"Yeah, every day. She has been my rock for this. She has been advising me about it, but it's hard without all the facts. She tells me to do my best. I try." He went silent.

"Can we look at the video again?" I asked.

Deacon gave me a nod and we went back to the break room. He said that Warren had taped the broadcast. He could tell by the record light on the VHS under the TV. He ran the tape back and played the video. We sat on a couple chairs and Deacon picked up the remote.

We watched the video again then ran it back and watched it again a couple times. I said, "I think the voice wasn't coming from the vigilante in the picture, his voice was too clear for someone speaking through a mask." Deacon agreed.

"Plus the camera followed the vigilante, so someone was taping the thing and giving the commentary," I said.

"Well, we already know there are two of them so it's not a surprise. We need to focus on each man. What do they have in common? Murder for purpose. What is their purpose? The vigilante said they were avenging a prior death, so it is a vendetta. What is that vendetta and how does it involve abuse and pimps?"

"Okay, taking the role of the killer, there was a case of abuse, some child, since it was years ago. Then the child becomes a prostitute as an adult and then was abused by a pimp. It fits so far. But now where does it go? If she was killed, the death of the child into woman hooker takes us where? To the courts? The vigilante made comments about the court system. Is he going after them now?"

Deacon just smiled as I said, "As much as I dislike lawyers and judges, do we have to protect them now?"

**

Chapter 23

"I wouldn't be upset if he went after a few lawyers. But putting my personal feelings aside, he hates abusers and pimps, and his innuendos say the legal system is included. Before long, he'll have all the people in Vegas on his list. This is getting too wide spread," I said.

"Yes, and if I don't find him, my ass is grass in this town."

"Hey, buddy, we'll catch him, one way or another. Have I ever let you down?"

"No, you haven't, and Lynn has said that a few times. So it must be true. Now can you help me catch this guy?"

"Would I not help? We now have to find the body of the guy in the video. I'm sure the vigilante will put him where everyone can find him."

Warren came back to the door and said, "The media didn't waste time putting your rant on screen, and they posted the picture of the suspect. We're now getting calls flooding the precinct."

"Get a couple men on taking those calls. Be sure to weed out the freaks and compile a list of the viable ones. Thanks, Greg." Deacon smiled at me. "Maybe we will find him or one of them yet."

Captain Weber snuck up to the door, startling Deacon and me, and wanted to talk to Deacon, alone. I could see Deacon starting to sweat. Deacon was the kind of person who liked to blend in the background. This was pulling him out of his comfort zone. He stood looking like he was going to the gallows and gave me a brave smile then went out to Weber's office. I sat at the desk and thought about the morning so far. My cell phone rang and caller ID said it was Penny.

"Yeah, babe, what's up?"

"Just wanted to say Jessie's first day at school went well. She says she already made a few friends, especially after they found out she was living with a famous P.I. and a talk show host. She'll be all right."

"Are we going to have to suffer with pajama parties now?" I asked.

"If it helps her to be popular in this school, it's fine with me."

"Hell, you'll be right in the middle of the party, won't you?"

"Damn right. I love a good pajama party. Speaking of which, I need to go out and buy some pajamas."

"You'll find any excuse to go shopping. Have fun, and we're starting to get some leads on the vigilante. I'll fill you in later. Oh, and buy some of those see-through p.j.s and a couple pairs of edible panties." She said I was disgusting and disconnected.

I had been sitting for about twenty minutes lost

in my thoughts when Deacon came back in smiling. "I presume you didn't get reamed out?" I said.

"No, the captain said confidentially that he loved what I had said, but he officially was giving me a reprimand for going to the press without talking to public relations first. I filled him in on our suspicions and he said to tread carefully in case it is a cop. Keep our heads low. I have to agree. A lot of these guys here are quietly rooting for the vigilante, and if it is a cop we'll have some resistance to catching him."

A detective I knew as Colin Parker came to the door with a sheet of paper. "Deacon, we had the computers burning up with your request for connections between abuse murders and cop family or friends. We narrowed it down to about eight hits." He handed the paper to Deacon and left.

Deacon studied the paper then looked at me. "Five of these cops are retired or out of service. The rest are still on duty. Shall we go hit the retirees first?"

I stood and said, "Are you still sitting?"

Deacon told Warren that we would be out for a while and we went to grab a car. I was holding the list and we decided to take them in order. First up was Mike Duffey who lived out in Valley View. I found the house on my Palm TX map program and we drove there. It was a nice house, desert landscaping, Spanish style building, looked well kept up. We got to the door as it opened and there stood a mountain of a man, muscles bulging through his t-shirt.

"Can I help you, Detective?"

Deacon registered a little surprise. "Are you Mike Duffey?"

"No, he's my father. What's this about?"

"I just need to ask him a few questions in regard to our investigation of the vigilante murders."

"He's not well and has trouble talking or remembering things for that matter. He has Alzheimer's and is getting feeble. Is it really necessary to talk to him?"

I could see past the man to his father sitting in a chair looking old. He turned his head to me and gave a weak wave. I looked at Deacon. He saw him also.

"Sorry to bother you. We don't need to talk to him. You take good care of him. He was a fine cop."

The man said thank you and we left.

Back at the car, I said, "We can rule him out. How did he know you were a detective?"

"Well, we pulled up in an unmarked police car, not much hiding that fact, and I look like a cop. Without a uniform, he figured I was a detective. Why didn't you deduce that?"

"I wanted to see if you could figure it out."

"Yeah, right." He smiled.

We spent the next hour and a half tracking down the rest of the retirees on the list. We found them to be overweight or dead. Deacon said he'd have to pull in the active duty cops now. It had to be done.

We drove back to Metro and put the car away. We entered the squad room and Warren came up and handed Deacon a pile of papers. "These are the hits we got so far on the phone calls. More are coming in."

"Where's Williams? He'd be good to follow up on these. Find him and tell him to take one other man just in case."

Warren went off and we went into Lynn's office. "So how is Lynn holding up?" I asked.

"She's actually enjoying the classes, or so she says. They are studying terrorists now. She said an attack on Vegas could happen, kind of like that movie where the terrorist was blowing up hotels and casinos."

He took the list of cops, picked up his phone and called the duty desk to ask if Officer Luke Fettering was on duty. He listened, asked if he could be paged and told to report to his office. He hung up and we made small talk while we waited. About ten minutes later a uniform cop came to the door.

"You wanted to see me, Detective?" He spoke softly.

"Yeah, Fettering, come on in and have a seat." He did. Then Deacon asked if he was aware of his case with the vigilante.

"Oh, sure, it's all over the place. You did good with those news people."

"Thanks. Can I ask you a few questions?"

He laughed and asked, "Should I have my lawyer and union rep here?"

"No, Luke. May I call you Luke?"

"Sure." He smiled.

"I'm aware of what you went through a few years back when your wife was murdered by persons unknown. Can you talk about it?"

"I've tried to get it out of my head, but it's not

easy. We were only married for a couple years. We were happy, a good marriage. I came home from work one night and found her dead. The killers were never found, not enough evidence." He looked angry.

"I hate to stir up bad memories, but I understand that your wife was an abused child."

"Are you asking if I have anything to do with the vigilante murders? I'm over it now. My wife is gone and I can't do anything to bring her back. As to the vigilante, I was on duty every time there was a killing. I'm quietly happy for his actions but I don't murder people."

"Thank you, Luke. We have to ask as you well know. I'm sorry to bring up the past."

"It's all right, Sarge. I'm a cop and I know the routine."

That was the first time I heard someone refer to Deacon by his rank. He made sergeant three months before. Deacon said Luke could leave and he went off.

Deacon called in the other two officers on the list and found out nothing more than the first. He was very discouraged and said so.

"What about North Vegas Police? Can you find any connection there?"

"Yeah, I'll call a friend later and see if he can do some hunting. We get a lead and then it goes sour. I'm hoping that the people who saw the sketch will turn up someone."

Deacon's phone rang and he answered, listened, said thanks and hung up. "We got a body." He stood and we went out.

153

Vegas Vigilante Murders

Traffic was light and we made good time going up Martin Luther King Boulevard to Lake Mead Boulevard and into Dolittle Park. We drove into the parking area, pulled over and noticed two patrol cars already there. Officers were taping off the area where the body was propped up on a park bench.

"Broad daylight and they drop him here. No cameras in the area, so they felt safe, I guess. Glad there weren't too many children here," Deacon said as the ME's SUV pulled up followed by the coroner van.

CSI rolled in and started to examine the area around the body. They pulled evidence and bagged it while Joe Lang checked the body.

Deacon stood looking at the cops on the scene and wondered. Could one of them have done this?

**

Chapter 24

I went to Deacon and said, "On the way here I was thinking."

"That's dangerous, you know," he interrupted.

"Thank you, I love you too. I was thinking about the murder of Kramer. Alicia Barnes said she saw the man tailing them, but how did he know what room they were in so he could pass the info to the vigilante? He would have had to be on the elevator to watch them go to their room, but video shows they were alone. So if he is a cop, could he ask at the front desk what room they were in?"

"Hotels aren't supposed to give out that

information but if he was a cop and he was persuasive, he may have gotten the room number." Deacon paused. I gave him time to think. "You know that may be a good lead. We should go to the Flamingo and do some inquiring."

I was proud of my student. I smiled. "That sounds like a good move. It gives us something to go on."

Deacon checked with CSI and Lang. They both said they were finished. Deacon said to me, "Let's go."

We drove back to Flamingo and into the parking structure at O'Shea's casino. After parking, we headed down to the street level and I stood in the alley looking towards the strip. I was running Trapper's report of his run-in with Alicia through my mind. Deacon came up and asked what I was doing.

"I'm just trying to recreate Trapper's meeting with Barnes. They went from parking to inside O'Shea's, then Trapper left her and went out to wait and see what she would do next." We arrived at the entrance to O'Shea's and I pointed to McDonald's next door. "He stood over there and waited. She came out with Kramer and they walked to the Flamingo and in to get a room. The killer had to have followed them but Trapper wasn't expecting them to be followed so he didn't see him."

We went into the Flamingo Hotel and up to the front desk. It was long and had about four stations for checking into rooms. Deacon went up, asked the clerk to see a supervisor, and showed his badge. The woman called someone on the phone and a few minutes later another woman came out.

"I'm Ms. Porter, shift supervisor. May I help you, officer?"

"That's Detective Sergeant DeAngelo, ma'am. I just need to ask a few questions."

"Certainly, what do you need? Is this about the murder on the fifth floor?"

"We think that a man pretending to be a LVMPD detective may have asked for the room of the victim and then may have committed the crime. I just need to know who may have been on the desk the day of the crime and if I can find out who may have given out that info."

"I understand what you want. I'll check the records and see who all were here and have them talk to you." She went off to a computer and started typing. She pulled a walkie-talkie and said something then came back. "Two of the girls are on the counter now and the other two are coming. I'll have someone replace the two here so you can take them all to a private room and talk to them."

"Thank you, Ms. Porter. When and if we get a hit, we'll need to see video of the incident. Think you can arrange it?"

"I'll talk to Dick in Security. I'm sure it can be arranged."

"Thank you," Deacon said as three girls came over to Porter, then another girl came up to the front of the desk. Porter told the girls to follow her and she waved to Deacon. We followed. She took us through a door and down a hall into a room.

Deacon introduced himself then me and asked

156

the girls to have a seat around the table.

"Okay, I'm not here to get anyone fired or arrest anyone, but we believe that one of you may have given out a room number to someone who may have identified himself as a police officer. Does this ring a bell?"

The four girls just sat silently. Ms. Porter spoke. "Someone talk or you will all end up on suspension!" Her bark made everyone in the room jump. It was still quiet then she said more quietly, "I'll give everyone a pass. Someone admit it and you all skate. The detective just wants to find the man who may have killed the guest on the fifth floor. Talk to him. I don't even want to know." She turned and went out the door.

The girls looked at each other and one girl cleared her throat. "I had a man who said he was a police officer. He even showed me his badge. He asked if the couple who just registered were the Kramers. I said they were, figuring he knew them by name, and he was a cop so it was okay. I'm sorry, I should have said something the day it happened but I was afraid I'd lose my job."

Deacon pulled out the sketch, slid it across the table and asked, "Is this the man you talked to?"

The girl looked at the picture and said, "It looks a lot like him. He had those weird sunglasses on."

I asked, "What kind of badge did he show you, the color of it?"

"It was a gold badge. I didn't see the ID very well, and he just flashed it quickly."

"Did he have any different way of talking, his

157

speech?" I asked.

"He had a deep voice, smooth and sounded intelligent, like he had good schooling."

"Anything else about him you can tell us?" Deacon asked.

"He was very nice. He had a nice smile. Other than that, he had nothing out of the ordinary to tell you. Did I get that man killed?" She was starting to tear up.

"No, you didn't, but never give out a room number without checking with your supervisor again. Even if he says he is a cop or FBI. Thank you for that."

Deacon asked if she remembered the time. She said it was around one in the afternoon, just after she got back from lunch. Deacon thanked all the girls and told them to go. They filed out and Ms. Porter came back in. Deacon said he got what he needed and requested she take us to the security office. She led us there and introduced us to Dick Chambers, the supervisor.

"Dick, we need to see surveillance footage from the day of the fifth floor murder, but at the front desk and around one o'clock."

He went to the controls, did some typing and then brought up the footage. We could see the girl clerk and a man in sunglasses showing her his ID. Deacon asked if he could get a few printouts of the scene and could they pull in to focus on his face. The man did a few things on the keyboard, went to a printer, and pulled the photos.

Deacon studied the pictures as I looked over his

shoulder. They weren't very good since the man kept his face down most of the time. But we had a body image now.

"Thanks, Dick, and you too, Ms. Porter," Deacon said. She led us back to the lobby of the hotel. We went out and back to our car.

Deacon was still studying the photos as we sat in the car. I said, "If we're going to sit here, could you at least put on the air conditioning? It's getting hot out."

He grinned and started the car. Driving out, he headed to Metro and along the way I asked, "Has Warren been able to locate any relatives for Jessie?"

"Oh, I forgot to mention it. I asked him that this morning. He said he can't trace a connection to anyone. The mother was an only child and the grandparents are both dead. The father had a brother but he was killed in Nam, and he left no family. Looks like Jessie is alone in the world."

I was feeling really sad then, thinking of my family back in Michigan. I couldn't visit them just anytime I wanted but I at least knew they were there. Jessie had no one. Penny and I had a decision to make.

Deacon said, "So we have another view of the killer. I'll get this out to the media and people can see we are doing something and making some progress. Maybe someone else remembers this guy from that day."

"Yeah, it may help. So far it's been quiet for further murders. I wonder what the boys are cooking up now?" I said.

Vegas Vigilante Murders

~~*~~

Attorney at law Peter Goerlich was leaving the county building happy in his thoughts of his triumph in court. He was able to get his client off on an assault charge. He was proud of his ability to manipulate the jury into what he wanted them to believe. He stood at his car when a man in narrow sunglasses approached him and carefully aimed a gun at his body.

"Mr. Goerlich, would you please accompany me, and don't make any quick moves. I'm good with this weapon."

Goerlich was weighing his options as a lawyer would do. He could stand his ground and get shot, go with the man and find out what that entailed or take a chance and jump the guy, possibly getting shot in the process. He took the least deadly way. He went with him. The man in sunglasses put the gun back where it wouldn't be seen and pushed the lawyer out to the end aisle of the parking lot. There was a tan van running at the end of the lot and the side door was open. The man in sunglasses pushed the lawyer towards the van and told him to get in. He did. The man slammed the door shut and looked around the parking lot. Seeing no one watching, he got into the passenger side. He turned to the driver, also in sunglasses and a hat, and said to drive. It was the last time anyone saw the lawyer alive.

**

Bob Moats

Chapter 25

We arrived at Metro and I told Deacon that I had a few things to do so I would join him the next day. He dropped me by my car and went to drop his car off. I got in my Crown Vic and called Lacey at the office. She answered.

"Richards Investigations, may I help you?" she said.

"Either you didn't look at the caller ID or you're being funny," I said.

She laughed and said, "I just wanted to show you that I do my job."

"I'm glad, and you do that so well. Have you heard from Penny lately?"

"She called about an hour ago and asked if you were in yet. I told her you weren't. She said she was going home and would see you there."

"Anything pressing going on?"

"Nope, it's quiet here. Trapper had a client in, but the client left and Trapper's getting organized to follow the errant wife. Buck is out checking the gas station guards. He's trying to keep them from shooting anyone."

"That's what happens when you hire bikers as guards. Well, I'm going home early for a change. I have to talk to Penny about Jessie. We can't find any relatives for her to go live with."

"I'd love to take her. She and I have been getting along real well. But you said I'd need to be married to Mac before that could happen."

I thought about that for about three seconds.

"Yes, that's something that we can look into. Have you and Mac talked about the wedding yet?"

"We did last night and it can be anytime with your generous offer to take care of the expense. We could do it soon and then Jessie could come live with us."

"How would Mac feel about having Jessie there?"

"He was disappointed when I told him about you asking me to take Jessie when we first met her but couldn't take her. He would love to take her now that he's gotten to know her."

"You'd have to get your own dog. I'm not letting Willy go."

I could hear her laugh, that sweet little laugh she could do. "I told Mac once before that I wanted a dog, especially while he was working midnights. He didn't object."

"Okay, I'll talk to Penny. You talk to Mac and we'll get this wedding on the move."

I arrived back home to find the girls in the pool, of course. Willy was swimming by Jessie. I sat on a plastic chair and Penny saw me, got out, and came over. She sat on a chair next to me and asked how my day was.

"Good. We're getting more evidence on our killers."

"You're not worried that they may branch out to average citizens?"

"No, they've stated their cause, and it's against a specific group of people. I'm not worried about your safety or Jessie's. Speaking of which, Warren can't find any relatives for Jessie, and I don't want her going to a foster home. I talked to Lacey and she is getting closer to marrying Mac and wants to take Jessie into their home. I think it would be a good move, considering their ages. What do you think?"

She sat quietly for a moment. "I would miss her being here, but I have to agree with you. We are getting on in years and later on it's going to be hard. I think about when Jessie is twenty, I'll be almost eighty. God, I hate the thought of being that old. I think it's a good idea."

"Why don't we tell her so she can prepare for it?"

She stood and went to the pool, calling Jessie to get out. Jessie came up the steps followed by Willy and over to us. I had pulled another chair to face us and asked her to sit.

I said, "Jessie, my police friends couldn't find a relative for you. Do you understand what that means?"

She looked sad and said, "Yeah, I got no family."

"Well, you better consider us your family now, and Lacey says that she would like to have you come live with her. Would you like that?"

"Can't I stay here?"

"We'd like that but you have to understand we are a lot older. It is hard with our jobs and we'll be getting older. Lacey is younger and can do more things with you. We could still have you come visit and stay with us when you want. And if Lacey and Mac want to do something, you could come and visit with us. We aren't giving you up, just sharing. Lacey and Mac would be like your parents and we would be your grandparents. How's that sound?"

Jessie sat thinking. She smiled and said, "Can I bring Willy with me?"

"No, Willy is our puppy, but Lacey mentioned she would get a dog too. Maybe they would let you pick one out," I said.

"Okay, that sounds good. I like Lacey and Mac. They treat me good and Lacey is funny and kind. When would this happen?"

"Well, Lacey and Mac have to get married first. I'm sure they would let you help with the arrangements." I looked at Penny and said, "Shall we call Shelby Francis to plan the wedding?" Penny smiled at the name of the wedding planner who helped us during the case of the Bridezilla murders and who planned our wedding.

"As long as there are no murders." She laughed.

"I'll call Lacey and Mac and have them come over to talk about it."

"I wish Lynn was here to help. She needs to start thinking about marrying Deacon."

I stood and said, "I'm going to my home office and make some calls. You two go back to playing." I left them and heard splashes back into the water.

I sat at my desk in my room set up for writing and hobbies and got on the home phone. I called Lacey.

~~*~~

Bob Moats

The room was semi-dark and Goerlich was handcuffed to a chair next to a desk. The man in the mask was sitting at the desk and called for the other man to start the trial. Goerlich was frightened now. The other man with the sunglasses was standing in front of him and said, "Your Honor, we find that this man, Peter Goerlich, has been derelict of his judiciary duties by allowing criminals to walk free and spit in the faces of the victims. He has helped a pimp to go free, allowing him to then murder one Kaylie Jean Duffey. His actions, in total disregard to humanity, have caused great hurt to Miss Duffey's family. He should be put to immediate death. Just like the way Miss Duffey was murdered. The prosecution rests."

Goerlich yelled, "Don't I get a say? I need a rebuttal. I need to defend myself!"

"Not in this court you don't. The way you twist words to suit your needs, not here. You are tried and found as guilty as the pimp you got freed to murder the judge's sister. Don't bother to speak. You aren't a lawyer here. Just the man found guilty." He turned to the masked man and said, "Judge, do your duty."

The masked man stood, came around front, put a revolver to the lawyer's head and pulled the trigger. The lawyer's head bounced backward then forward, dropping down to his chest.

"Justice is almost finished," the masked man said and pulled his mask off.

~~*~~

Vegas Vigilante Murders

Around seven o'clock Lacey and Mac arrived at our home along with Shelby Francis, the wedding planner. We all went to the family room and sat.

I spoke first. "Well, after spending a bit of time on the phone, I have called everyone together to get Lacey and Mac hitched."

Lacey was bouncing. Jessie was sitting next to her with Willy on her lap. Next to Jessie, Mac was grinning widely and then I asked, "Shelby, you did so well with Penny's and my wedding, I called you to arrange a shotgun wedding for our friends here. Think you are up to the challenge?"

She smiled and said, "Your wish is my command."

"Good. Lacey and Mac want to wed this Saturday so they can take a nice honeymoon and then come back to start a family." I looked at Jessie and smiled. "It's been all arranged. The newlyweds will fill out the paperwork to be foster parents and, if all goes well, Jessie will have a good home."

Mac rustled Jessie's hair and said, "It will be a good home and we're taking Jessie to get her own dog. Not that we don't like Willy, but he belongs here."

"So, Shelby, get with the youngsters and start the procedure." I went to Penny who was standing by the door and kissed her. "Honey, our kids are getting married."

Everyone had left after plotting out the wedding in four days. It would be tight but doable. I called Deacon and told him. He was happy and said he'd be there. I called Buck and he wanted to have a bachelor party for Mac, complete with strippers. I said he'd better check with Mac before he did that. Trapper said he'd attend and asked if he could bring Sam, his bookie girlfriend. I said he could. I came out from my room and found Penny sitting on the couch with Jessie and Willy watching our wedding DVD video that was recorded by Penny's station back in Detroit. That was the week that we endured the Bridezilla murders.

I hoped everything would go well this time.

**

Chapter 26

I woke early when Deacon called. He was apologetic but said I might like what he had to say. A lawyer was found dead by the hand of the vigilante. I wasn't fond of lawyers but I didn't want them dead at the hands of killers. I found out the details of the murder and told Deacon that I would be there in a while. I got up and went to wake up in the shower. I was a little surprised to suddenly find a body next to me. It was Penny. She said we needed to conserve water. I didn't object.

We toweled off and Penny went to dress to go into her show while I made breakfast for Jessie and me. Penny went off to work and I got Jessie out the door to the school bus. She was happy that she was going to live with Lacey and Mac. I got Willy ready for Lacey to pick him up.

I had everyone off to work, school or

babysitting, and drove to meet Deacon at the county building. I parked and found him standing out front of the main building near a body covered by a tarp.

"Good morning," he said.

"So you say. What's the deal?"

"Lawyer, Peter Goerlich, was shot point blank in the head, stripped naked of his clothes and dumped here in front of the courts and the rest of the sharks. It was a warning."

"Anyone see the dump?"

"They did it early this morning before everyone was ready for the day. Surveillance cameras show the dump but don't show the perps. A van pulled up quickly, the side door opened, he was pushed out, and the van sped off. We'll probably find this van, wiped clean, parked behind another vacant building like the other one they used for the pimp. I'm now getting calls directly from the mayor's office to get my ass in gear and catch this guy or guys."

The meat wagon rolled up and Joe Lang stepped out. "Sorry I'm late but the bus broke down in the middle of the strip. I had traffic backed up all the way down to the Monte Carlo. So what we got?"

Deacon pulled the tarp back enough to show Lang the body. The ME went to the form on the ground and started his exam. The uniformed cops had taped off the whole front of the building to keep people back enough so not to see too much. People were gathering to see what was going on. The media was just arriving in full force and being obnoxious. Cameras and reporters lined the tape to get a scoop or sound byte.

Bob Moats

I stood on the side with Deacon. He wasn't happy. "Okay, this lawyer gets it. Why him? Was he part of the vendetta they were waging for the death of some woman? Maybe if you put him along with the pimp and abusers, maybe there is a connection," I offered to him, hoping it might help.

"Yeah, it might. I'll put Warren in charge of this and we'll go back and run the info." He called to Warren who just showed up and told him to take charge as we went to our cars.

We arrived at Metro and Deacon was ducking Weber. He didn't want to explain this morning's death. We went into Lynn's office and Deacon closed the blinds so we'd have a little privacy. He sat at his computer and pulled up the file on the pimp, Wolfie Dupree. He sat reading, occasionally out loud for my sake, and then saw it.

"Yep, Wolfie was represented by Peter Goerlich in an assault charge two years ago. Goerlich got Wolfie off due to a technicality in the arrest, and he was freed." Deacon read some more. "Now six months later Wolfie is arrested for suspicion of murdering one of his women, and again it's Goerlich who reps him. The trial lasted two weeks and Goerlich managed to establish reasonable doubt to get Wolfie freed again. I'm not liking Goerlich."

"Who was the murdered victim?" I asked.

"Doesn't say here, but I can pull that record." Just as he said that, the door opened and Weber was standing there looking depressed.

"Sergeant DeAngelo, we need to talk." He walked away.

Vegas Vigilante Murders

Deacon quietly said, "Damn," then went out after Weber. I sat alone in the room wondering if this was going to bode well for Deacon.

I went around to the computer and was looking at the file Deacon had on the screen. I wasn't supposed to be snooping in those files, but I wanted something to go with. Most of it I couldn't understand due to codes and cop speak that I really needed to learn, but I got the general idea.

Goerlich was Wolfie's lawyer and got him freed, then Wolfie went out and murdered a hooker. Was that the woman that the vigilante was trying to avenge? It made sense. Now if we could get the name of that woman, it might lead us to the killer. I was sitting back when the door flew open startling me from my thoughts. It was Deacon. He wasn't smiling but he wasn't frowning either.

"The captain gave me one more chance to catch the killer before another death. Jim, I'm not happy. The vigilante is on a killing spree and I haven't much to go on."

"Well, try and find out who the murdered prostitute was and maybe we will find the killer," I said, hoping it might help his mood. I got up from Lynn's chair as he came around the desk and sat.

He did some typing and hit a few keys that made the screen glow brighter. He sat reading and looked at me with a surprised expression. "Kaylie Duffey," was all he said.

I thought back and the name was familiar. Then it came to me. It was the same last name as the first cop we went to see, Mike Duffey, the man with

170

Alzheimer's. The man who had a very big son we hadn't talked to. I could see Deacon's wheels spinning. He smiled and said, "Let's go see Mike Duffey again."

We went out and took a car then drove back to the Duffey residence. When we got to the door, no one answered. Deacon was trying to see in the windows off the porch but the house looked empty. Deacon pulled his cell phone and called for an APB on the son, Steven Duffey, for suspicion of murder. He didn't say that he believed him to be the vigilante, but that would come out later. We walked around the house and found nothing extraordinary, just standard things you'd find around a house. Deacon looked in the back window of the garage and didn't see a car. They had to be out, he said.

"Let's go back and pull the case file on Kaylie Duffey to see what we can find," Deacon said and we left.

When we arrived back at Metro, Deacon headed straight to Weber's office to tell him of his finding, hoping to placate the captain. I sat in the office until he came in smiling. "Weber remembers the case and said it was a good lead. He's happy for now. We just need to find Duffey." Deacon sat down and typed some more, came up with the case file and read the brief form.

"It seems that one of Wolfie's arresting officers was reprimanded for a minor act of violence against the suspect. It turns out to be Mike Duffey." Deacon was reading from Duffey's sheet, and he said, "Duffey was given a suspension but turned in his papers for retirement shortly after citing medical reasons. They list him as having early stage Alzheimer's."

As he was reading, some strange looking guy in a suit came to the door. "Sergeant DeAngleo, I'm Larry Fenero, public liaison for the department. We need to get a statement, official this time, to the press. We've set up a press conference at one this afternoon, so please have a statement ready and let me know what you are going to say so I can approve it." He said he'd be back and walked off.

"That was quick," I said.

"Department heads want to please the public. They'll spin this to their favor, hopefully not using my hide to hang out. What I told the captain was a real good lead, so the captain is covering his butt with his bosses."

Deacon sat back in the chair, probably formulating his speech in his head. I just sat watching him when my cell phone rang. I said I would take it out in the squad room. I went out and over by the windows looking out to the world then answered after seeing it was listed as private. I didn't like those calls but answered it anyway.

"Hello?" I said and heard a familiar voice. It was Shelby Francis. "Hi, Shelby, what's up?"

"I've got a quickie but good wedding planned for your friends. It will come to a little over two thousand dollars, and I wanted to check with you to see if that is doable."

"That sounds good, make it so," I said sounding like Captain Picard from Star Trek. She laughed and

172

said that she would stop by my office around three that afternoon to talk to Lacey, Mac and me about the arrangements. I told her I would have everyone there and we hung up.

Things were taking shape and I was feeling good. I went back to Lynn's office and Deacon was gone. I looked around and saw him talking to Williams. I waited.

He came back to me and said, "They found Mike Duffey, the father. He's in a nursing home over in Henderson. No sign of Steve Duffey. He's hiding out."

"He must have figured we'd pick up on him after the Goerlich murder. Was Steve ever a cop?"

"No, he was a bodybuilder and trainer at a gym over on Decatur. Williams called the gym and they say he hasn't been in for days. They don't know where he could be."

Warren came in and said they had Goerlich on ice and they found a note stuck in his mouth. Deacon read the copy, "This is what happens to big mouth lawyers. The vigilante."

**

Chapter 27

Larry Fenero came back as promised and listened to Deacon's statement, edited it a bit then approved it as written. He escorted Deacon to the front of the building where they had set up a podium which the media had plastered with microphones.

Vegas Vigilante Murders

Deacon had never been the focus of one of these press conferences. Lynn always was the speaker for the department, and she looked good on camera.

The press conference went well. Deacon gave his edited statement about who was the major suspect at large for the vigilante murders and showed a picture that they took off the internet from his gym. The captain made a statement, then the commissioner of police summed it up and closed the conference by saying there would be no questions. That didn't please the press but they had enough to feed the public.

It was a waiting game now. The release of Duffey's photo and the fact that he was connected would probably make him go underground. I told Deacon that I had a wedding to plan and if anything came up to call. I left the station and drove back to my office.

I came in to a lobby full of men all talking at once. They were Buck's guards. I got the drift that they were congratulating Mac and Lacey as the young couple sat on chairs by Lacey's desk. She was surrounded by presents, probably from the guards. Buck was standing by the hallway door grinning, I went to him.

"I suppose this is your doing?"

"I thought they should have a wedding shower with the gang. I gave them tickets to anywhere they want to go for their honeymoon since you're paying for the wedding. I don't want to look cheap." He grinned his walrus smile and we watched the festivities.

174

Bob Moats

Trapper came in the back door and I went to his office following him. "Are you on the case of the bad girl wife?"

"Yep, I got some good photos of wifey and her boy-toy. Enough for hubby to file for divorce. What's going on up front?"

"It's a wedding shower for Mac and Lacey. They're getting married Saturday, but you know that since you are invited. Is Sam coming with you?"

"Yep. We are getting along very well now," he said with a smile.

"Is she still taking book or gone legit for you?"

"No, she still has her bookie operation. As long as she keeps it on the low, the cops won't bother her. I put in a good word with a few of the command officers who just happen to use her services."

"You just love bending the law, don't you?"

"Only if it suits my needs."

Buck came back and said there was a woman to see me. I figured it was Shelby. I went up front, invited Shelby to my office, and asked Mac if he and Lacey could come in for our talk. They came back and Buck sent his men back to work. Everyone was happy.

About ten minutes later Penny came in, wondering where everyone was, and went straight to my office. She pulled up a chair and we talked about the wedding for the next hour and finalized it all. The wedding was to be held at the same chapel where Penny and I were married, and there would be no Elvis preacher. Shelby had a real minister coming in. That pleased Penny, remembering our wedding.

Vegas Vigilante Murders

Mac still had family in Vegas so they had about twenty people total invited for the reception. In all there would be about fifty people attending. We signed papers for the arrangements and then I asked Mac if they got the license yet. He gave me a strange look and said, "Damn, we forgot."

I told them to take the rest of the day and take care of it. He and Lacey went off as Penny and I sat with Shelby, talking about old times.

~~*~~

"You knew if we exposed Goerlich and Wolfie that the cops would figure it out," Duffey yelled to his partner from the other room. "They've shown my picture and I can't go out now. This is something I didn't think about. They'll be watching my father. I can't even go see him now. I do not like this."

"Don't worry. I'll take care of your father. We can disguise you so you can at least go out in public. You knew the risk. This was a pact to avenge your sister, and we have done that except for one last person. We'll take care of him later. We'll just lay low for now and let it die out. One more kill and you have finished your objective."

"Maybe so, but I'm not happy about killing a cop, even if he deserves it."

~~*~~

I took Penny out for a nice sit down lunch and then we went to pick up Jessie from the bus stop. We went back to the house and the girls went off to swim. Willy followed Jessie to the pool and they were having a good time. My cell phone rang and it was Deacon.

"Don't tell me there was another murder."

"Nope, it's been quiet so far. I think our exposé this morning may have slowed them down. Lynn called and she's flying in for Lacey and Mac's wedding. She's staying just the day and then back to Quantico. It'll be good to see her even for a day."

"Great, I'll tell Penny. So no word on Duffey, eh?"

"Nope, we have been checking all the places he frequented according to his friends and co-workers. I have almost twenty men out canvassing the city. He's going to have to go deep."

"Do you need me now? I'd like to spend some time with my girls."

"No, I don't. we pretty much have it now. But I really thank you for the push you've been giving. it helped."

"Don't mention it. I'm always glad to help you anytime."

"I'll keep you informed as to any developments. Talk later."

He hung up and I went to my home office, sat at the laptop, and worked on my latest book. Sales were very good for my first book and the second was coming out next month with good reviews so far. The money was starting to come in from sales and I was pleased. My bank account was still flowing from all my past cases and the sales so I was able to do the things I wanted, like giving Lacey and Mac a good wedding.

I was having a good time in my own little world typing on the keyboard when my cell phone rang. It was Lacey. "Yeah, Lacey, did you get the license?"

"Yes, we did, and we are good to go," she replied.

"Great. Now we have five days to go before the celebration, so get ready and no more sex till the wedding night," I joked.

She giggled. I could almost see her blushing through the phone and then she said she'd be good. I hung up and looked out to the pool through my window. Penny was stretched out on the lounger as Jessie and Willy sat nearby playing. All was good in our lives. I just wondered about Steve Duffey and his purpose for avenging his sister. Would I go that far if Penny were murdered? How much would I be willing to lose for her?

I occasionally give some murderers the benefit of the doubt for what they do. Except the psychopaths, they are hardwired in their brains to be bad. I didn't have any sympathy for them. But are they responsible for their actions if they can't control what they do? Cold-blooded killers are mentally ill, that's my feeling. They're not right in the head to do what they do from abusing people to torture and murder. It's a strange world. I don't take it for granted though. I have to be careful being out in the world, but I can't obsess over it either.

Now I knew that Steve Duffey was avenging his sister and taking out a few bad guys. Well, lawyers may be rotten but not bad enough to murder. Should I give sympathy to Duffy? He wasn't a bad person, just frustrated into committing murder. How far can a person be pushed before they snap? "Going postal" was a catch phrase for snapping at your job. It happens a lot around the world. Push someone too hard, they can push back. Or shoot back.

I sat in my thoughts until I saw Penny and Jessie gathering up towels and heading in. I went out to the kitchen and waited while they changed. I pulled a DiGorno Pizza out of the freezer and popped it into the oven. Then I took out a bag of chips and put them in a bowl. I was getting ready for movie night at the Richards' house.

We watched a scary movie on cable and then everyone went off to bed. I took a couple of beers for Penny and me and we went into our bedroom, ready to hit the sheets. We relaxed with the TV on, watching late night talk shows. Nothing good on so we shut it off and snuggled.

"I'm going to miss Jessie when she goes," Penny said quietly.

"I know. I've grown to like her too. But she would be happier with Lacey and Mac. We're too wrapped up in our own interests to be parents. I have a busy enough life as it is. So do you. After she goes we'll see if we survive. We can still always adopt a child if we are too lonely."

179

"You can always bring home another stray. You're good at that." She grinned and cuddled closer.

We slept well that night.

**

Chapter 28

Wedding: four days and counting.

I stood at the bathroom mirror and thought about coloring my hair and beard. I was looking old. Maybe a little touch up so not to look like those men who dye their hair jet black and wear sunglasses to hide the bags under their eyes. There was Botox or a face-lift, but I wasn't that vain. Penny passed by my door and then came back to see what I was staring at. I told her.

"You look fine. I like the way you look. Don't go changing." She sounded like a recording. "Staring won't make you look better. I'll have my make-up people give you a makeover. Then we'll see if it helps." She went off to get ready for work. I stopped staring.

Penny had gone off and I got Jessie out to the bus stop, then I drove to the office with Willy sitting in the passenger seat. I had his leash tied to the seat belt clamp to keep him from jumping around.

I parked out front and took Willy in, finding the front lobby empty. I went to Buck's office, also empty, then to Trapper's, still empty. I was standing there wondering where everyone was when the back door opened and in came Trapper.

"What's going on?" I asked.

"We were admiring the new cars for Buck's security. Two cute little Vibes, like Lynn's car."

"I didn't know the firm had two new cars," I said and went to the back door.

In the back parking lot by our office was Buck, Lacey, Mac and a few of Buck's guards standing looking at the cars. They had signs on the side announcing "Richards Security and Investigations" and flashers on top.

I came up to Buck who was grinning. "When did this happen?" I asked.

"I had them delivered this morning. Nice, huh?" he said like a proud father.

"Yes, nice. I know we talked about this, I just didn't think it would be so soon."

"Well, the dealership we are guarding made a great offer. They're used cars and the price was right. So I bought them."

"Okay, it's something we agreed on, so enjoy your new toys," I said and looked them over. They were in good shape and clean. Low mileage and the tires looked new. I gave Buck a thumbs up and went back in the office.

Lacey followed me and went to her desk. Trapper was in his office writing up his report for the man whose wife was cheating on him. He made up a file complete with glossy photos. I went in and sat, watched him poring over the file and coughed. He looked up and said, "Can I help you?"

"Nope, just killing time. I'm a little bored now that Deacon has someone for the vigilante."

"He hasn't been caught yet, so it's not over. You still have to deduce where he may be."

"LVMPD has approximately 300 investigators with more than 100 civilian support personnel assigned to catch criminals. Deacon is a cog in a big wheel. He has help to catch Duffey now. I just helped steer him in the right direction. I need a new case to work on. It's too slow." I watched him sit back and stare at me. "Maybe I'll put your face on the billboards we have. You might bring in a few more clients," I said, referring to the two billboards that featured Buck and me looking tough.

"Don't even think about putting me on a billboard. I don't photograph well. I'll call in a few markers and see if I can stir up a good divorce case for you just to get you out of my office," he said with a smile.

I stood and said, "Fine, I'll go sulk in my office." I went out and to the lobby.

Lacey was sitting sorting out papers for Buck's security schedules. I stood at the counter until she realized I was watching her. "What? Did I do something wrong?"

"No. You have a guilty conscience, don't you?"

"Yes, you know that, but you keep standing watching me. It's creepy."

I never thought of me as creepy. "I'm sorry, I'm bored. Don't we have any cases?"

"None yet, just the one Trapper took the other day."

"Okay, I'm going out to stir up some trouble," I said and went out the door to my car. I was going to bug Deacon.

I arrived at Metro and found Deacon was out tracking down Duffey and wouldn't be back for a while. I thanked the desk officer and went back to my car. It was still early so I went to take a drive up the strip and kill some time before I went to lunch.

I checked my phone to be sure it was on and it was. If Deacon needed me, he would call. I went over to Charleston and Maryland and went into my favorite store back when I was poor and needed cheap food. It was the Grocery Outlet. Back when I first lived out there with my son, before I met Penny, we would come in once a week and buy our provisions for the week. Those were fun times.

I bought some fruits even though I didn't eat them much and got some veggies and frozen foods. Penny never liked to shop for groceries even though she was a shopaholic. I usually did the grocery shopping. I threw everything in the car and drove back home.

I put the groceries away and thought I should have brought Willy with me. I'd call Penny to pick him up. I looked at the couch in the living room. It was calling my name. I sat at first and then stretched out and, shortly after, was asleep.

I was being tapped on the head, pulled out of a nice dream about being admired by throngs of people for my books. I forced my eyes open and looked up. It was Penny tapping my head. Jessie was standing behind her holding Willy. I forced my body to get up and sat looking at the women looking at me.

"I was tired," I defended. "I look old and feel old."

Penny laughed and sat next to me. "I still love you even if you are old." Jessie went to her room after saying we were being silly.

"Am I silly?" I asked Penny.

"A goof ball, yes, but silly, no."

"I was bored today. I wish it was Saturday so we could get into the wedding."

"It'll be here before you know it. Now just relax. Why don't you go work on your book?"

I thought of the options and it sounded the best. I stood. "I got you some fresh fruit today."

"Thank you, sweetie. Now go have fun."

I went to my room and worked on my book until Penny came in and said she had dinner ready. We ate and then crashed on the couch to watch television and enjoy our beer and snacks. Jessie was online chatting with some new friends from school and she was where we could see her. I knew enough about computers, the web and chat rooms, so I was careful about what she did online while she was still with us. She was good about it and I knew she could be trusted. Besides, she had friends now.

We pooped out around eleven o'clock. Jessie was asleep on the easy chair so we put her to bed and went to our room.

"So what did you do exciting today?" Penny asked.

"I rescued a damsel in distress and saved a bunch of tourists from a terrorist threatening to blow up a casino and was bored the rest of the day."

She giggled and said she could believe that. We fooled around for a short time then went to sleep.

Next morning I got Penny off to work and Jessie to school then I fed Willy so my day was starting well. I called Lacey and told her not to pick up Willy. We were going to spend the day together, a little male bonding. Lacey thought I was cracking up. I said I was. She laughed and hung up. I was sitting at my desk typing my story on the laptop. Willy was on the chair next to me watching with his head down.

I thought about Duffey and wondered what he was up to then an idea came to me. I saved my story to disk, then flipped my virtual desktop over to another screen and brought up the Opera browser to get online. I wanted to see if there were any stories about the Kaylie Duffey murder on the internet, so I brought up Google and typed in her name.

I had all the usual hits for Kaylie and then Duffey, even using the quote marks. People think if they use the quote marks they'll get the exact match. Well, it usually worked but they always threw in a good number of wrong hits to pump up the ratings.

I dug through the search pages and found an article about the case written by a freelance reporter for the Vegas Sun newspaper. It was more of an exposè about the way the case was handled by the police and the courts. I read the article. It was written through an interview with Steve Duffey. He blamed the lawyers and the police for not following procedure in the case. Wolfie was let off from assault charges because the lawyer, Peter Goerlich, brought up discrepancies in the arrest of Wolfie. That allowed Wolfie to go free to commit the murder of Kaylie. She was one of his girls and Wolfie didn't like the way she did her business or so Duffey believed.

Duffey said he blamed the lawyer and the police for her death. He singled out one cop for his hate. A name that gave me a chill.

**

Chapter 29

I read the rest of the story. It seemed that Wolfie Dupree was originally arrested for assault on Kaylie who was working as one of his girls. The police hauled him in but never gave him his proper rights, plus they beat up on him, or so the lawyer said in court. It wasn't brought up that Wolfie was strung out and resisted arrest. I figured that the lawyer probably twisted the incident to his way. Wolfie got off on the charges and two days later Kaylie was found dead. The police again arrested Wolfie as the prime suspect and again Goerlich got him off on technicalities. Seems the arresting officer didn't follow the proper procedures to get evidence on Wolfie, no search warrant, so the weapon was inadmissible and the case was thrown out due to lack of evidence.

I called Deacon when I finished the story. I was printing it out as he came on. "Where are you at?"

"I'm in Lynn's office. What's up?"

"I may have something for you. Wait there," I

said and hung up. I grabbed Willy's purse, put him in it, took the story I printed from the printer and left. I stopped by the office, dropped off Willy and said I was hot on the trail of the killer. Lacey said it was about time. I didn't have time to debate with her and left.

I got to Metro and into Lynn's office where I found Deacon just sitting. I handed him the paper and told him to read. He did. He finished and looked at me, shaking his head.

I said, "I think the other vigilante is the reporter. He does mention that he is going to do a book about the incident. What better way to pump up a story than to get the characters into trouble?"

Deacon sat looking at the paper and then looked at me. "Duffey says he blames the cop who did the bust for sloppy and negligent police work. Allowing the criminal to be freed to kill his sister."

"Yes, and you see who that cop is."

Deacon read from the paper, "Officer Bernie Williams."

We both looked out to the squad room to where Williams was sitting, using the phone.

Deacon stood, went to the door and called Williams. He finished and came to the room. "What's up, Sarge?" he said.

Deacon asked him to have a seat and then handed him the paper. Williams read the first paragraph and put it down. He looked sick. "I tried to forget that happened. I was treated poorly after that. Sergeant Mike Duffey made my life hell, so I transferred out from North Vegas and came here. I tried to put it all behind me. I wasn't thinking straight back then. I wanted the bust so bad to show I wasn't a fool like everyone thought I was. I regret it all now."

"Why didn't you say something when you heard it was Steve Duffey we were after?"

"I thought it wouldn't come up. I hoped we would find him and it would all go away. When the old man started having his Alzheimer's attacks, I figured it would go away." He looked at the paper. "I didn't know some reporter was dragging it back up."

"Yeah, and he probably pushed Duffey into being the vigilante. You are on that short list of people who are being murdered."

Williams gave Deacon a strange look and asked what he meant.

"Abusers were murdered. Kaylie was abused, her pimp Wolfie Dupree was murdered, now Peter Goerlich has been taken out for letting Wolfie walk. You are one of the links to that incident. Think about it. You may be next."

Williams sat in disbelief and then said, "What should I do?"

"I'll assign you protection but you have to be careful now. Go see Warren and I'll have him put a detail on you. I won't give details as to why you are being singled out but I'm sure some of these people know."

"Thanks, Sarge." He stood and went out.

"Shall we go find this reporter?" Deacon said.

"Call the Vegas Sun to see if they have his address," I said.

He nodded and pulled out his address book,

looked up the newspaper, dialed a number and asked to speak to Harry Estaban. He waited and then said, "Harry, it's Deacon DeAngelo. How are you doing?" He listened and then asked if Harry could give him the address of a Benjamin Latham, a freelance writer. He waited, then wrote something on a pad of paper and thanked Harry. He looked at me and said, "Let go bag a bad guy."

We drove up to Owens Avenue, west of Civic Center Drive just before it turned into Eastern Avenue. We found the house in a subdivision and pulled up. Deacon called a friend in North Vegas PD and asked if he could get some backup. We sat waiting and then a patrol car rolled up behind us. Deacon got out and explained that we weren't sure if this guy was one of the men we wanted, but to be careful. The two cops said they'd be ready for anything.

Deacon told me to hold back and took one of the officers with him. They went to the door. Deacon banged on it and waited. There was no response. Deacon and the cop went around the house and looked in the windows but saw nothing. Deacon wished there was some reasonable cause to enter the building without a search warrant, but remembered Williams' attempt to do the same thing. He didn't want to taint the scene.

Deacon came back, called the DA and explained what we needed. He was told to wait. We stood talking about the case until Deacon's phone rang and he was told a warrant was issued and was on the way. One of the cops called for more backup and Deacon called for CSI to stand by. About twenty minutes later an assistant of the DA drove up with the warrant. He said the judge was more than happy to push it through due to the nature of the case. Probably worried he'd be next for the vigilante.

The backup had arrived and Deacon plotted out the move. They went to the house and Deacon banged again, yelling that it was the police and to open up or they would enter with a warrant. He did it mostly as a matter of procedure. They brought up the battering ram and the door went down. The cops flowed into the house. I waited for the place to be cleared.

I stood at the door as I heard the clear call made a number of times. I carefully went in. Deacon was standing in the kitchen as I came up and asked if they found a basement. Deacon turned to the back door and saw stairs going down. He called a couple of men to go with him. They went down the stairs and Deacon smiled. He saw the chair, blood all over the back wall, and it was the same basement that he had viewed on the murder video. He called CSI and told his men they had a crime scene.

CSI had finished gathering as much evidence as they could find and left. The house was quiet after the North Vegas police had gone back to their precinct. Deacon and I stood in the basement looking around the room. It was chilling to think this room was used for the murder of Wolfie and Goerlich. I was taking it all in when I heard a noise from behind the wall. I thought it might be a mouse, but then I heard a stifled sneeze. Mice don't sneeze. I knew that. I tapped

Deacon and pointed to the wall. He heard it also. I went to the paneling that covered the wall and looked carefully for an opening. Deacon had drawn his weapon as I saw a tab and grabbed it. I nodded to Deacon just as the wall fell downward pushing Deacon and me to the floor. I was under the paneling and Deacon's head was just over the top of the wood. He was not moving. He had a gun in his face.

We were both tied to chairs as Benjamin Latham stomped around. "You damn people had to push this. Couldn't just let us scrub the city of the stink that pervades our town. This won't do and now you have seen me. I can't write my book and get away with this if I let you live. Crap, I had it all planned. I was going to waste Duffey as a good citizen and be the hero. My book would sell millions. Maybe even make a movie out of it."

I laughed. "That's not as easy as it looks."

"Shut up!" he said and paused. "But you may come in handy yet. I'll use your gun to kill Duffey and shoot you with his, and that will be that. As soon as Duffy gets here with Williams, it will be over."

"What makes you think he'll get Williams here?"

"Duffey called him and said he wanted to give up and wanted Williams to take him in. But he had to be alone. Duffey told Williams that he was afraid of the cops, that they might kill him. Williams agreed to come, last I heard."

We were startled by a loud noise and saw the body of Williams come rolling down the stairs. Behind him came Duffey.

He had a gun aimed at Latham. "I heard it all,

Vegas Vigilante Murders

Benny. You thought you would kill me. Oh no. I'm going to kill you. I got Williams and that is the end of it all, but your death will make it all the more perfect. You taught me to be a killing machine, so it won't bother me to take one more life." He aimed higher and pulled the trigger. The gun exploded and Latham went down. Duffey turned to me and said, "Sorry, guys, but I can't let you live either. Latham will take the fall for all this. I'll clean it up and make sure it looks like he was the vigilante. Sorry, guys, nothing personal." He was bringing up his gun towards Deacon when we heard another explosion. It came from Warren's gun as he was standing on the bottom step of the stairs. Duffey went down and Warren came to us, bringing his pocketknife out to cut our ropes.

"How did you find us?" Deacon asked.

"I put a tracker on Williams. We followed that." He went to Williams, checked him and said he was alive. More cops flowed into the room from the stairs. I was never so glad to see cops. "Williams gave us the slip. He wanted to bring in Duffey by himself. He wanted to prove himself, but he's Williams, just can't get it right."

**

Chapter 30

Saturday morning finally arrived. I had spent the last three days hiding out, relaxing from the ordeal that Deacon and I went through. Williams was being released from the hospital. Warren told everyone that Williams volunteered to be taken by the vigilante so we could capture him. Deacon and I were the only other people who knew the truth but we weren't talking. Williams was a screw-up but he needed this, a little retribution for past screw-ups.

Lacey and Mac were spending the morning getting ready for their wedding. The night before Buck threw a bachelor party for Mac complete with strippers. They were well behaved. The men, that is. Deacon and I enjoyed ourselves, even if Deacon was given a number of lap dances. Lacey went out partying with Penny, Maria and Lynn who flew in a day early, delighting Deacon. They came back a bit drunk and Lacey was suffering for it that morning according to Penny, who was a bit sick herself. Lynn came out of it unscathed. She had a good constitution for drinking.

Shelby was with the girls in our guesthouse, busy getting Lacey into her dress. Shelby wanted to take care of this wedding herself with help from just one of her employees. The fitting of the dress two days ago and it fit fine then, but Lacey was now struggling to be tucked into the dress. She admitted she put on a little weight by eating too much the last two days. She was nervous. They managed to squeeze her in but then she had to stand until the wedding or she might pop out.

We had reserved a banquet hall at the Silver Dollar Casino and Hotel where Lacey had worked and she still had a little pull with the banquet people so we got a nice discount. The room was all decorated by the women who worked with Lacey and they were invited to the reception, bringing the cost up a bit more, but what the hell, it was their day too.

Deacon drove up to our home and I let him in. Lynn came in from the guesthouse and latched onto him, giving kisses that bordered on obscene. He was grinning. I knew he got a lot of loving the night before.

I had pulled our mini-limo, the one from the mob family in New York, out of the garage and parked it out front. The ceremony was to be held at noon, and we were ready to go. I asked Jessie to take care of Willy. She put him in his purse and was walking around with the dog hanging his head out.

Mac was at Buck and Maria's house getting ready. Buck was Mac's best man, I was giving the bride away, and Penny was the maid of honor. Maria was going to take pictures with her new digital camera that Buck bought her. Jessie was going to be the flower girl and Willy was going to be in the procession too.

Lacey was ready and we went out to carefully put her in the limo. I drove the women up to the chapel where Penny and I were wed. It was good to see the place again. I went into the chapel and it was filled. I was surprised. I hoped they weren't all coming to the reception.

I went back to find Mac and Buck in the groom's room. Mac was ready to faint. That was funny for such a big, macho man, but a wedding can do that to you.

Warren came in, pulled Deacon to the side and said that the case was officially closed, everything was filed away and the press was given the story, or at least what we wanted them to know. Then Warren went out to sit in the chapel.

The procession was about to start. Mac had asked a couple close friends to stand up with him, and Lacey asked a few of her former co-workers to stand up for her. Mac was standing by the altar as the wedding march began and I brought Lacey down the aisle. We arrived at the altar and I gave Lacey to Mac then went to sit in the front pew next to Jessie who did a great job spreading the flowers.

The ceremony went well, it was over and we all filed out doing the throwing of the birdseed at Penny's insistence. I drove the couple around Vegas in the limo and they were hooting and hollering in the back. I opened the roof and let them stick out and wave at all the people on the strip. The limo was decorated and looked the part of the wedding vehicle so people knew what was going on. I drove up to the Silver Dollar, dropped them off at the door and parked.

The reception was fun and happy. Lacey threw the bouquet and it was caught by Lynn who cast an eye toward Deacon. We celebrated for a couple hours then Mac took Lacey to their car and went off. I sat at a table with Penny, Buck, Maria, Deacon, Lynn, Trapper and his date, Sam. I wished the newlyweds well and we toasted for the tenth time.

Penny was getting tipsy and frisky. I knew I was going to get lucky that night.

The next day Mac and Lacey went to Hawaii for their honeymoon and came back a week later, worn out from the trip. I had them in the office of CPS the following day where they finished filling out the papers they started before the wedding to certify them as foster parents. Jessie was bouncing around, happy for her new home. Doris Braco was happy that we had placed Jessie in a good home and then we went to get Jessie's things to take to Mac and Lacey's home. Penny and I finished moving things to their house and said our good-byes. They said they were going to the local animal shelter to get a dog for Jessie.

We drove home and Penny was quiet most of the way. I asked, "Are you all right?"

"I'm just happy and yet a little sad that Jessie's gone."

"But you'll see her regularly. We are the grandparents and have to babysit frequently," I said.

"You can be her grandfather, I'll be her favorite aunt," she said and leaned over Willy to give me a big kiss on the cheek.

**

The End

Bob Moats

For every ending, there's a new beginning.

~~*~~

Preview chapter of "Area 51 Murders"

Chapter 1

The razor wire was meant to cut into the skin of any person trying to escape over the fence. It was doing its job on Darryl's arms, body and legs as he tried to go over the fence to get out from the U.S. military's base 85 miles north of Las Vegas, the infamous Area 51.

Darryl didn't care so much that his body was being shredded by the sharp coils of metal atop the fence; he just wanted to escape from the insanity of what he had witnessed in the restricted area that the government denied existed. He was now being followed by forces, ones who wanted him to stay in the compound, and to be a guinea pig for their experiments. Not something he wanted to be subjected to.

He fell to the ground on the free side of the fence; but was suddenly surrounded by military personnel holding their high-powered rifles and handguns on him. He laid there frustrated by the men who had no thoughts of what he went through in the secret base, which very few people on earth had any concept of what was actually going on there. He just laid back and let them take him. Screw it, he thought, he now didn't care.

Vegas Vigilante Murders

~~*~~

Richards Investigations was gaining a little notoriety from its involvement in the Vigilante murders case. The police commissioner had given me his thanks publicly for my aid in finding the killer, so now I was being sought out to solve all kinds of cases. I didn't mind it, but at sixty-two years, I didn't want to become overworked now. I actually enjoyed the slow pace days back before the press made a big deal out of it. I had enough money in the bank from my book sales and I really didn't need to work hard if I didn't want to. Being a private eye was fun for me, but now it was becoming work.

My beautiful and sometimes odd wife Penny slapped my butt, telling me to get my ass out of bed. I pulled the pillow over my head and tried to ignore her, but she's not one you can ignore. She grabbed on the sheets and gave a good pull, exposing me to the harsh reality of Sunday morning. She left our bedroom and went off into the house to plot her day, followed by Willy, our toy Yorkie.

I pulled myself up and forced myself to the shower where I put on the cold water by mistake and nearly froze my still sleeping body, a definite eye-opener. I toweled off and throwing on a robe, went to the kitchen. Penny was eating her usual morning bowl of oatmeal as I put my two pieces of bread in the toaster.

"What wondrous things are we going to do today?" she asked between spoonfuls of mush.

"I haven't given it a thought," I said as I was trying to coax the toaster to accept the bread, it just kept popping up before it toasted the slices. "Between the two of us, we have enough money to buy a new toaster. You love shopping let's go buy one." I said before realizing what I said.

Her eyes lit up on that thought, she finished the last bite of her oatmeal and said, "I'll get ready, the mall is calling." She went off as I regretted initiating a shopping trip. I didn't mind shopping now that I had money to buy silly things, but shopping with Penny was work for me.

The house phone rang and I hoped it would spare me from a trip to the mall. "Hello?" I said.

It was Lacey, my office manager slash receptionist. She had recently married Mac, the supervisor for my friend and partner Buck's security guard business. The two of them took in and adopted Jessie, the nine-year-old whose abusive father was murdered by the vigilante and then Penny and I had her for a couple weeks before she went with Lacey and Mac.

"I hope you are calling to say there's a big case needing my attention," I said hopefully.

"Why, does Penny have something for you to do?"

"Shopping," I said.

"Oh, well I could make something up to get you out of it."

"No, that all right. What's up?"

"Mac and I are having a backyard barbeque next weekend and wanted to invite you and Penny."

Vegas Vigilante Murders

"I'm sure we can make it. How's married life?"

"We're doing well and Jessie is a joy to have with us. Mac is starting to spoil her; I have to be the bad guy when they start plotting."

"Enjoy every minute of it. My son grew up so fast it was as if it never happened. I'll tell Penny about your BBQ and I'll see you at the office tomorrow morning."

"I'll be there after I get Jessie off to school." She said as we finished our call.

Penny came back in and asked who was on the phone, I thought about telling her it was a case needing my immediate attention, but she always knew when I was fibbing. She had this telepathy that I couldn't avoid.

"It was Lacey; we're invited to a BBQ next weekend at their home."

"Good, we can see Jessie again. So shall we go attack the mall?"

I was grinning but feeling dread. "Sure, off to buy a new toaster."

We went to the garage to get my car and headed to the huge mall a couple miles from our home on the far western edge of Las Vegas. The view from our house of the Vegas valley and the tall buildings of the Vegas strip, made our home worth living in. We attacked the mall, or I should say Penny attacked the mall; I just kept up with her. We found a big toaster in Macy's that I was sure could make the bread, toast and butter it all at one time, so we bought it. I was fulfilled, but Penny was still raring to go.

Half of our shopping time was usually spent with

Penny being recognized for her morning TV talk show and having to stop and talk to her fans. No one recognized me; I was just Penny's husband. After about three hours of shopping and lunch in the food court, we headed back home.

We spent the rest of the day relaxing; Penny swam in the pool most of the day while I was in my home office typing on the keyboard trying to finish my third book about the Dominatrix murders back in Michigan. Willy was lounging by the pool, I guess he had enough of swimming by himself, and I think he missed Jessie.

Buck called me to say he picked up another car dealership for his guards. He mentioned about a body found up by Area 51, everyone was saying he was murdered by aliens.

"Buck, there would be no body if aliens killed the guy, they would disintegrate him with their death rays, leaving only a dust pile." I said.

"Well, the people up there say they saw strange lights and heard loud noises coming from where the body was dumped. That's how they found him, they followed the lights. I tell you it was little green men."

"Why are they always little green men, why not chartreuse, an off green color that would give them a little fashion sense. And why little, are they munchkins from over the rainbow?"

"Now you're being silly. They're not munchkins; they're from outer space, not Oz."

"Maybe so, but I'm not going to worry about it. Are you going to be in the office tomorrow?"

"I'll be there early to get the paperwork ready for

the new job. I'll probably be there when you get in."

"Okay, see you in the morning, and don't get abducted by little green men."

"Now you're making fun of it. I do believe in them."

"I do too; I just don't think they would murder someone and dump the body."

"Okay you have a point. See you tomorrow," He said and hung up.

I looked out my window and saw Penny was sunbathing by the pool now on her stomach, her bikini top was off and she was looking at me looking at her. I waved and she flashed me her naked breasts and then dropped back down, laughing. For a fifty-nine year-old woman she still had a great body and was still beautiful. Her youthful look helped for her talk show, which was doing well in the ratings since she started here. I did miss the days back in Michigan when she would bring odd things home from her talk show there, and drive me crazy with them. My best memory was when she was made up to look like Marilyn Monroe by the drag queens she had on her show, I got to take Marilyn to bed with me. It was nice.

I went back to my story just as my cell phone rang, the caller ID said it was Deacon.

"Hey big guy, what's up." I said.

"You read a lot of books don't you?" he said.

"Yes, I have read a good number, why?"

"You ever read science fiction stories?"

"Sure, Ray Bradbury was my favorite author along with H. G. Wells. Again, why?"

"Did you read the Sunday Review-Journal this morning?" He asked as I remembered that I forgot to pick-up the paper.

"No, is there some big crime in it that needs my attention."

"Well, there was a murder out by Area 51 that may need looking into. I got a call from some woman who was married to the victim, she called me because it was said that I knew you, she was looking for you to find her husband's killer."

**

Continued in the book.

~~*~~

Jim Richards Family of Readers

Thanks to the following people who are now part of the Jim Richards Family of Readers. They have read a book or more and enjoyed them. They all volunteered to be included in the list. If you are a fan of the books, send me your full name and you will be included in future books. Send your name to murdernovels@bobmoats.com to be added here and on the website.

* Achim Feifel * Al Norris * Alex Wheatley * Alexandra Delporte-Wilkinson * Amy Tapia * Andrea Bryan * Anne Shepherd * Arianda Sugar * Arlene Markowski * Ashley Augustus * Audra Hall * Barbara Hughes * Barbara Sammons * Barbara Schuler * Barbara Zirger * Beth Donohue Plenskofski * Betsy Childress * Beth Gibson * Bill Sandy * Bill Tornquist * Billie-jo Collie * Boni J Rychener * Carl Bishopric * Carla Lewis * Carole Henderson * Carolyn Conroy * Carolyn Riddle-Linington * Cassy Bailey * Cathie Turner * Chad Hudson * Charlotte L Duran * Cheryl L. Everett * Cindy Ackley Nunn * Cindy Valstad * Connie Bancroft * Corinne Kay O'Daniel * Dana Robbins Chuchran * Dana Wichita * Danielle Monique * Darren Heald * Dave Travers * David Wilkinson * DeAnn Jannereth * Deanna Miller * Deb Breuker Balbo * Debbie Carter * Debbie White * Deborah Fartuch * Deborah Gauze * Deborah Sullivan * Dee King * Denise Freeman * Diana Carver * Dixie Beck * Donna Gould * Donna Thompson * Donny Minter * Doris Kight

Bob Moats

* Eddie Moore * Eric Walters * Felicia Annette Bradfield * Francine Menor * Gail Chesney * Georgiann Minster * George Conner * Greg Colucci * Hayley Rankin * Harold Garcia * Heidi Arnold * Irma Ranee Coy * Jacqueline Moss * Jan Kimball * Janice Schneider * Janice Spoor * Jennifer Redmond * Jessica Keown-Belous * Jim Beck * Jo Boguslaw * Jo Turner * Joanne Marie Turner * John Peiffer * John Wisbiski * Joseph Wauro * Joyce Stacy * Joyce Trifiletti * Judy Franklin * Judy Travers * Judy Padgett * Julie Heath * Junnahvee Benson * Karen Dahl * Karen Grams * Karen Higham * Karen Kaiser * Karen Meinburg Richwine * Karen Kirkman Parker * Karin Hawkins * Karin Vasvari * Kathleen Donohue Roesing * Kathleen Riddle-Wolfe * Kathy Hinds Moore * Kathy Jones * Kathy Mitchell * Katie Benzler * Kay Burns * Kelly Garcia * Ken Boggs * Keota Rodriguez * Kiera Mccarthy * Kim Estes * Kitty Stolle * Kristie Sciler * Kirsty Stanton * LaLonnie Scallen * Larry Morris * Leann Parr * Lenora Scales * Leslie Marie Jackson * Linda Forester * Linda Ingle Cox * Linda Kennerö * Linda Magill * Lisa Bower * Liz Gibson * Lorraine Wiman * Loretta Alexander * Lynda Bowles * Lynette Lawrance * LuAnn Louttit * Manny Rothman * Marcia Gibson DeWitt * Marie Calder * Marlene Bryan * MaryLouise Kramp * Mary Lynn Gross * Megan Atkins * Meghan Hyden * Melody Cannavan * Michael Carruthers * Michael Dinkens * Michael Vannoy * Michelle Burns-Mitchell * Michelle Pilcher * Micki Potter * Mike Moats * Mimi Baur * Myrna Hecht * Nadine Sutton * Nancy Ellen Sayre * Natalie Quine * Neena Martin * O'Della Wilson * Pat Pollington * Pat Rohn * Patricia Jarmon * Patricia C Trezza * Patrick Barry * Paul Lawrance * Peggy Davis * Phyllis Bassett * Raylene Matheny * Rebecca Collins Besner * Renee Brumley * Reta Hanna * Reta Moats * Roberta Navarro-Harder * Sally Berneathy *

Vegas Vigilante Murders

Sally Hubler * Sarah Santos * Satka Nikc * Sharon E. Edwards * Sharon Mangini * Sharon McMillon * Sheena Rawl * Sherry Amstutz * Shirley Alvarez * Shirley Davies * Shirley Williams * Stacie Rowe * Stephanie Conner * Steve Cullen * Susan Haughton * Susan Hesse Adams * Susan Salomon * Suzan K Chase * Taisha Cullum * Tamara Moore * Tammy Castleberry * Tammy Lynn Wood * Ted Murphy * Terri Atkins * Terri Creech * Terry Raab * Tonia Rachael Riggs-Williams * Travis Fleury-Lopez * Twyla Gawlas * Val Brooks * Walt Munsel * Yvonne Isakson *

Thank you to all these wonderful people.

Thank you for purchasing this book. I hope you enjoy it as much as I enjoyed writing it for my faithful readers. Please feel free to email me to tell me what you thought about my stories. I love hearing from the readers. I can be reached at murdernovels@bobmoats.com thanks again!